DEMIAN / *The Story of Emil Sinclair's Youth*

HERMANN HESSE

DEMIAN

The Story of
Emil Sinclair's Youth

Buccaneer Books
Cutchogue, New York

Introduction

A FULL DECADE has passed since I last shook Hermann Hesse's hand. Indeed the time seems even longer, so much has happened meanwhile—so much has happened in the world of history and, even amid the stress and uproar of this convulsive age, so much has come from the uninterrupted industry of our own hand. The outer events, in particular the inevitable ruin of unhappy Germany, both of us foresaw and both lived to witness—far removed from each other in space, so far that at times no communication was possible, yet always together, always in each other's thoughts. Our paths in general take clearly separate courses through the land of the spirit, at a formal distance one from the other. And yet in some sense the course is the same, in some sense we are indeed fellow pilgrims and brothers, or perhaps I should say, a shade less intimately, confreres; for I like to think of our relationship in the terms of the meeting between his Joseph

Knecht and the Benedictine friar Jacobus in *Glasperlen-spiel* which cannot take place without the "playful and prolonged ceremony of endless bowings like the salutations between two saints or princes of the church"—a half ironic ceremonial, Chinese in character, which Knecht greatly enjoys and of which, he remarks, Magister Ludi Thomas von der Trave was also past master.

Thus it is only natural that our names should be mentioned together from time to time, and even when this happens in the strangest of ways it is agreeable to us. A well-known elderly composer in Munich, obstinately German and bitterly angry, in a recent letter to America called us both, Hesse and me, "wretches" because we do not believe that we Germans are the highest and noblest of peoples, "a canary among a flock of sparrows." The simile itself is peculiarly weak and fatuous quite apart from the ignorance, the incorrigible arrogance which it expresses and which one would think had brought misery enough to this ill-fated people. For my own part, I accept with resignation this verdict of the "German soul." Very likely in my own country I was nothing but a gray sparrow of the intellect among a flock of emotional Harz songsters, and so in 1933 they were heartily glad to be rid of me, though today they make a great show of being deeply injured because I do not return. But Hesse? What ignorance, what lack of culture, to banish this nightingale (for, true enough, he is no middle-class canary) from its German grove, this lyric poet whom Moerike would have embraced with emotion, who has produced from our language images of purest and most delicate form, who created from it songs and aphorisms of the most profound artistic insight—to call him a "wretch" who betrays his German heritage simply because he holds the idea separate from the form which so often debases it, because he tells the people from whom he sprang the truth which the most dreadful experiences still cannot make them understand, and because the misdeeds committed by this race in its self-absorption stirred his conscience.

If today, when national individualism lies dying, when no single problem can any longer be solved from a purely national point of view, when everything connected with the "fatherland" has become stifling provincialism and no spirit that does not represent the European tradition as a whole any longer merits consideration, if today the genuinely national, the specifically popular, still has any value at all—and a picturesque value may it retain—then certainly the essential thing is, as always, not vociferous opinion but actual accomplishment. In Germany especially, those who were least content with things German were always the truest Germans. And who could fail to see that the educational labors alone of Hesse the man of letters—here I am leaving the creative writer completely out of account—the devoted universality of his activities as editor and collector, have a specifically German quality? The concept of "world literature," originated by Goethe, is most natural and native to him. One of his works, which has in fact appeared in America, "published in the public interest by authority of the Alien Property Custodian, 1945," bears just this title: "Library of World Literature"; and is proof of vast and enthusiastic reading, of especial familiarity with the temples of Eastern wisdom, and of a noble humanistic intimacy with the "most ancient and holy testimonials of the human spirit." Special studies of his are the essays on Francis of Assisi and on Boccaccio dated 1904, and his three papers on Dostoevski which he called *Blick ins Chaos* (*Glance into Chaos*). Editions of medieval stories, of novelle and tales by old Italian writers, Oriental fairy tales, *Songs of the German Poets,* new editions of Jean Paul, Novalis, and other German romantics bear his name. They represent labor, veneration, selection, editing, reissuing and the writing of informed prefaces—enough to fill the life of many an erudite man of letters. With Hesse it is mere superabundance of love (and energy!), an active hobby in addition to his personal, most extraordinarily personal, work—work which for the many levels of thought it touches and its concern with the problems of the world and the self is without peer among his contemporaries.

Moreover, even as a poet he likes the role of editor and archivist, the game of masquerade behind the guise of one who "brings to light" other people's papers. The greatest example of this is the sublime work of his old age, *Glasperlenspiel,* drawn from all sources of human culture, both East and West, with its subtitle "Attempt at a Description of the Life of Magister Ludi Thomas Knecht, Together with Knecht's Posthumous Writings, Edited by Hermann Hesse." In reading it I very strongly felt (as I wrote to him at that time) how much the element of parody, the fiction and persiflage of a biography based upon learned conjectures, in short the verbal playfulness, help keep within limits this late work, with its dangerously advanced intellectuality, and contribute to its dramatic effectiveness.

German? Well, if that's the question, this late work together with all the earlier work is indeed German, German to an almost impossible degree, German in its blunt

refusal to try to please the world, a refusal that in the end
will be neutralized, whatever the old man may do, by
world fame: for the simple reason that this is Germanic in
the old, happy, free, and intellectual sense to which the
name of Germany owes its best repute, to which it owes
the sympathy of mankind. This chaste and daring work,
full of fantasy and at the same time highly intellectual, is
full of tradition, loyalty, memory, secrecy—without being
in the least derivative. It raises the intimate and familiar
to a new intellectual, yes, revolutionary level—revolutionary in no direct political or social sense but rather in a
psychic, poetical one: in genuine and honest fashion it is
prophetic of the future, sensitive to the future. I do not
know how else to describe the special, ambiguous, and
unique charm it holds for me. It possesses the romantic
timbre, the tenuousness, the complex, hypochondriacal
humor of the German soul—organically and personally
bound up with elements of a very different and far less
emotional nature, elements of European criticism and of
psychoanalysis. The relationship of this Swabian writer of
lyrics and idyls to the erotological "depth psychology"
of Vienna, as for example it is expressed in *Narziss und
Goldmund*, a poetic novel unique in its purity and fascination, is a spiritual paradox of the most appealing kind.
It is no less remarkable and characteristic than this author's attraction to the Jewish genius of Prague, Franz
Kafka, whom he early called an "uncrowned king of German prose," and to whom he paid critical tribute at every
opportunity—long before Kafka's name had become so
fashionable in Paris and New York.

If he is "German," there is certainly nothing plain or
homely about him. The electrifying influence exercised on

a whole generation just after the First World War by *Demian*, from the pen of a certain mysterious Sinclair, is unforgettable. With uncanny accuracy this poetic work struck the nerve of the times and called forth grateful rapture from a whole youthful generation who believed that an interpreter of their innermost life had risen from their own midst—whereas it was a man already forty-two years old who gave them what they sought. And need it be stated that, as an experimental novel, *Steppenwolf* is no less daring than *Ulysses* and *The Counterfeiters?*

For me his lifework, with its roots in native German romanticism, for all its occasional strange individualism, its now humorously petulant and now mystically yearning estrangement from the world and the times, belongs to the highest and purest spiritual aspirations and labors of our epoch. Of the literary generation to which I belong I early chose him, who has now attained the biblical age, as the one nearest and dearest to me and I have followed his growth with a sympathy that sprang as much from our differences as from our similarities. The latter, however, have sometimes astounded me. He has written things— why should I not avow it?—such as *Badegast* and indeed much in *Glasperlenspiel*, especially the great introduction, which I read and feel "as though 'twere part of me."

I also love Hesse the man, his cheerfully thoughtful, roguishly kind ways, the beautiful, deep look of his, alas, ailing eyes, whose blue illuminates the sharp-cut face of an old Swabian peasant. It was only fourteen years ago that I first came to know him intimately when, suffering from the first shock of losing my country, my house and my hearth, I was often with him in his beautiful house and garden in the Ticino. How I envied him in those days! —not alone for his security in a free country, but most of all for the degree of hard-won spiritual freedom by which he surpassed me, for his philosophical detachment from all German politics. There was nothing more comforting, more healing in those confused days than his conversation.

For a decade and more I have been urging that his work be crowned with the Swedish world prize for literature. It would not have come too soon in his sixtieth year, and the choice of a naturalized Swiss citizen would have been a witty way out at a time when Hitler (on account of Ossietzky) had forbidden the acceptance of the prize to all Germans forevermore. But there is much appropriateness in the honor now, too, when the seventy-year-old author has himself crowned his already rich work with something sublime, his great novel of education. This prize carries around the world a name that hitherto has not received proper attention in all countries and it could not fail to enhance the renown of this name in America as well, to arouse the interest of publishers and public. It is a delight for me to write a sympathetic foreword of warm commendation to this American edition of *Demian*, the stirring prose-poem, written in his vigorous middle years. A small volume; but it is often books of small size that exert the greatest dynamic power—take for example *Werther*, to which, in regard to its effectiveness in Germany, *Demian* bears a distant resemblance. The author must have had a very lively sense of the suprapersonal validity of his creation as is proved by the intentional ambiguity of the subtitle "The Story of a Youth" which may be taken to apply to a whole young generation as well as to an individual. This feeling is demonstrated too by the fact that it was this particular book which Hesse did not wish to have appear over his own name which was already known and typed. Instead he had the pseudonym Sinclair—a name selected from the Hölderlin circle—printed on the jacket and for a long time carefully concealed his authorship. I wrote at that time to his publisher, who was also mine, S. Fischer in Berlin, and urgently asked him for particulars about this striking book and who "Sinclair" might be. The old man lied loyally: he had received the manuscript from Switzerland through a third person. Nevertheless, the truth slowly became known, partly through critical analysis of the style, but also through indiscretions. The tenth edition, however, was the first to bear Hesse's name.

Toward the end of the book (the time is 1914) Demian says to his friend Sinclair: "There will be war. . . . But you will see, Sinclair, that this is just the beginning. Perhaps it will become a great war, a very great war. But even that is just the beginning. The new is beginning and for those who cling to the old the new will be horrible. What will you do?"

The right answer would be: "Assist the new without sacrificing the old." The best servitors of the new—Hesse is an example—may be those who know and love the old and carry it over into the new.

Thomas Mann

April, 1947

I wanted only to try to live in accord with
the promptings which came from my true self.
Why was that so very difficult?

DEMIAN / *The Story of Emil Sinclair's Youth*

I cannot tell my story without reaching a long way back. If it were possible I would reach back farther still—into the very first years of my childhood, and beyond them into distant ancestral past.

Novelists when they write novels tend to take an almost godlike attitude toward their subject, pretending to a total comprehension of the story, a man's life, which they can therefore recount as God Himself might, nothing standing between them and the naked truth, the entire story meaningful in every detail. I am as little able to do this as the novelist is, even though my story is more important to me than any novelist's is to him—for this is my story; it is the story of a man, not of an invented, or possible, or idealized, or otherwise absent figure, but of a unique being of flesh and blood. Yet, what a real living human being is made of seems to be less understood today than at any time before, and men—each one of whom represents a unique and valuable experiment on the part of nature—are therefore shot wholesale nowadays. If we were not something more than unique human beings, if each one of us could really be done away with once and for all by a *single bullet, storytelling would lose all purpose. But every man is more than just himself; he also represents the unique, the very special and always significant and remarkable point at which the world's phenomena intersect, only once in this way and never again. That is why every man's story is important, eternal, sacred; that is why every man, as long as he lives and fulfills the will of nature, is wondrous, and worthy of every consideration. In each individual the spirit has become flesh, in each man the creation suffers, within each one a redeemer is nailed to the cross.*

Few people nowadays know what man is. Many sense this ignorance and die the more easily because of it, the same way that I will die more easily once I have completed this story.

I do not consider myself less ignorant than most people. I have been and still am a seeker, but I have ceased to question stars and books; I have begun to listen to the teachings my blood whispers to me. My story is not a pleasant one; it is neither sweet nor harmonious, as invented stories are; it has the taste of nonsense and chaos, of madness and dreams—like the lives of all men who stop deceiving themselves.

Each man's life represents a road toward himself, an attempt at such a road, the intimation of a path. No man has ever been entirely and completely himself. Yet each one strives to become that—one in an awkward, the other in a more intelligent way, each as best he can. Each man carries the vestiges of his birth—the slime and eggshells of his primeval past—with him to the end of his days. Some never become human, remaining frog, lizard, ant. Some are human above the waist, fish below. Each repre-

sents a gamble on the part of nature in creation of the human. We all share the same origin, our mothers; all of us come in at the same door. But each of us—experiments of the depths—strives toward his own destiny. We can understand one another; but each of us is able to interpret himself to himself alone.

1) Two Realms

I SHALL BEGIN my story with an experience I had when I was ten and attended our small town's Latin school.

The sweetness of many things from that time still stirs and touches me with melancholy: dark and well-lighted alleys, houses and towers, chimes and faces, rooms rich and comfortable, warm and relaxed, rooms pregnant with secrets. Everything bears the scent of warm intimacy, servant girls, household remedies, and dried fruits.

The realms of day and night, two different worlds coming from two opposite poles, mingled during this time. My parents' house made up one realm, yet its boundaries were even narrower, actually embracing only my parents themselves. This realm was familiar to me in almost every way —mother and father, love and strictness, model behavior, and school. It was a realm of brilliance, clarity, and cleanliness, gentle conversations, washed hands, clean clothes, and good manners. This was the world in which morning hymns were sung and Christmas celebrated. Straight lines and paths led into the future: there were duty and guilt,

bad conscience and confession, forgiveness and good resolutions, love, reverence, wisdom and the words of the
Bible. If one wanted an unsullied and orderly life, one
made sure one was in league with this world.

The other realm, however, overlapping half our house,
was completely different; it smelled different, spoke a
different language, promised and demanded different
things. This second world contained servant girls and
workmen, ghost stories, rumors of scandal. It was domi-
nated by a loud mixture of horrendous, intriguing, fright-
ful, mysterious things, including slaughterhouses and
prisons, drunkards and screeching fishwives, calving cows,
horses sinking to their death, tales of robberies, murders,
and suicides. All these wild and cruel, attractive and
hideous things surrounded us, could be found in the next
alley, the next house. Policemen and tramps, drunkards
who beat their wives, droves of young girls pouring out of
factories at night, old women who put the hex on you so
that you fell ill, thieves hiding in the forest, arsonists
nabbed by country police—everywhere this second vigorous world erupted and gave off its scent, everywhere, that
is, except in our parents' rooms. And that was good. It was
wonderful that peace and orderliness, quiet and a good
conscience, forgiveness and love, ruled in this one realm,
and it was wonderful that the rest existed, too, the mul-
titude of harsh noises, of sullenness and violence, from
which one could still escape with a leap into one's mother's lap.

It was strange how both realms bordered on each other,
how close together they were! For example, when Lina,
our servant girl, sat with us by the living-room door at
evening prayers and added her clear voice to the hymn,

her washed hands folded on her smoothed-down apron,
she belonged with father and mother, to us, to those that
dwelled in light and righteousness. But afterwards, in the
kitchen or woodshed, when she told me the story of "the
tiny man with no head," or when she argued with neighborhood women in the butchershop, she was someone
else, belonged to another world which veiled her with
mystery. And that's how it was with everything, most of
all with myself. Unquestionably I belonged to the realm
of light and righteousness; I was my parents' child. But
in whichever direction I turned I perceived the other
world, and I lived within that other world as well, though
often a stranger to it, and suffering from panic and a bad
conscience. There were times when I actually preferred
living in the forbidden realm, and frequently, returning to
the realm of light—necessary and good as it may have
been—seemed almost like returning to something less
beautiful, something rather drab and tedious. Sometimes I
was absolutely certain that my destiny was to become like
mother and father, as clear-sighted and unspoiled, as
orderly and superior as they. But this goal seemed far
away and to reach it meant attending endless schools,
studying, passing tests and examinations, and this way led
past and through the other, darker realm. It was not at all
impossible that one might remain a part of it and sink into
it. There were stories of sons who had gone astray, stories
I read with passion. These stories always pictured the
homecoming as such a relief and as something so extraordinary that I felt convinced that this alone was the right,
the best, the sought-for thing. Still, the part of the story
set among the evil and the lost was more appealing by far,
and—if I could have admitted it—at times I didn't want

the Prodigal Son to repent and be found again. But one didn't dare think this, much less say it out loud. It was only present somehow as a premonition, a possibility at the root of one's consciousness. When I pictured the devil to myself I could easily imagine him on the street below, disguised or undisguised, or at the country fair or in a bar, but never at home with us.

My sisters, too, belonged to the realm of light. It often seemed to me that they had a greater natural affinity to my father and mother; they were better, better mannered, had fewer faults than I. They had their faults, of course; they had their bad moments, but these did not appear to go very deep as they did with me, whose contact with evil often grew so oppressive and painful, and to whom the dark world seemed so much closer. Sisters, like parents, were to be comforted and respected; if I had quarreled with them I always reproached myself afterwards, felt like the instigator, the one who had to ask for forgiveness. For by offending my sisters I offended my parents, all that was good and superior. There were secrets I would far rather have shared with the lowest hoodlum than with my sisters. On good days, when my conscience did not trouble me, it was often delightful to play with them, to be good and decent as they were and to see myself in a noble light. That's what it must have been like to be an angel! It was the highest state one could think of. But how infrequent such days were! Often at play, at some harmless activity, I became so fervent and headstrong that I was too much for my sisters; the quarrels and unhappiness this led to threw me into such a rage that I became horrible, did and said things so awful they seared my heart even as I said them. Then followed harsh hours of gloomy regret

and contrition, the painful moment when I begged forgiveness, to be followed again by beams of light, a quiet,
thankful, undivided gladness.

I attended the Latin school. The mayor's son and the
head forester's son were in my class; both visited me at
home at times, and though they were quite unruly, they
were both members of the good, the legal world. Yet this
did not mean that I had no dealings with some of the
neighborhood boys who attended public school and on
whom we usually looked down. It is with one of them that
I must begin my story.

One half-holiday—I was little more than ten years
old—two neighborhood kids and I were roaming about
when a much bigger boy, a strong and burly kid from
public school, the tailor's son, joined us. His father drank
and the whole family had a bad name. I had heard much
about Franz Kromer, was afraid of him, didn't at all like
that he came up to us. His manners were already those of
a man and he imitated the walk and speech of young
factory workers. Under his leadership we clambered
down the riverbank by the bridge and hid below the first
arch. The narrow strip between the vaulted wall of the
bridge and the lazily flowing river was covered with nothing but refuse, shards, tangled bundles of rusty wire and
other rubbish. Occasionally one could pick up something
useful here. Franz Kromer instructed us to comb the area
and show him what we found. He would either pocket it
or fling it into the river. He put us on the lookout for
objects made of lead, brass, and tin, all of which he
tucked away—also an old comb made of horn. I felt very
uneasy in his presence, not only because I knew that my
father would not have approved of my being seen in his

company, but because I was simply afraid of Franz himself, though I was glad that he seemed to accept me and treat me like the others. He gave instructions and we obeyed—it seemed like an old habit, even though this was the first time I was with him.

After a while we sat down. Franz spit into the water, and he looked like a man; he spit through a gap between his teeth and hit whatever he aimed at. A conversation started up, and the boys began boasting and heaping praise on themselves for all sorts of schooolboy heroics and tricks they had played. I kept quiet and yet was afraid I'd be noticed, that my silence might particularly incur Kromer's wrath. My two friends had begun to shun me the very moment Franz Kromer had joined us. I was a stranger among them and felt that my manners and clothes presented a kind of challenge. As a Latin school boy, the spoiled son of a well-to-do father, it would be impossible for Franz to like me, and the other two, I felt acutely, would soon disown and desert me.

Finally, out of sheer nervousness, I began telling a story too. I invented a long tale about a robbery in which I filled the role of hero. In a garden near the mill, I said, together with a friend, I had stolen a whole sackful of apples one night, and by no means ordinary apples, but apples of the very best sort. It was the fear of the moment that made me seek refuge in this story—inventing and telling stories came naturally to me. In order not to fall immediately silent again, and perhaps become involved in something worse, I gave a complete display of my narrative powers. One of us, I continued, had had to stand guard while the other climbed the tree and shook out the apples. Moreover, the sack had grown so heavy that we had to open it again, leaving half the apples behind. But half an hour later we had returned and fetched the rest.

When I had finished I waited for approval of some sort. I had warmed to my subject toward the end and been carried away by my own eloquence. The two younger ones kept silent, waiting, but Franz Kromer looked sharply at me out of narrowed eyes and asked threateningly:

"Is that true?"

"Yes," I said.

"Really and truly?"

"Yes, really and truly," I insisted stubbornly while choking inwardly with fear.

"Would you swear to it?"

I became very afraid but at once said yes.

"Then say: By God and the grace of my soul."

"By God and the grace of my soul," I said.

"Well, all right," he said and turned away.

I thought everything was all right now, and was glad when he got up and turned to go home. After we had climbed back up to the bridge, I said hesitantly that I would have to head for home myself.

"You can't be in that much of a hurry." Franz laughed. "We're going in the same direction, aren't we?"

Slowly he ambled on and I didn't dare run off; he was in fact walking in the direction of my house. When we stood in front of it and I saw the front door and the big brass knocker, the sun in the windows and the curtain in my mother's room, I breathed a sigh of relief.

When I quickly opened the door and slipped in, reaching to slam it shut, Franz Kromer edged in behind me. In the cool tiled passageway, lit only by one window facing the courtyard, he stood beside me, held on to me and said softly:

"Don't be in such a rush, you."

I looked at him, terrified. His grip on my arm was like a vise. I wondered what he might have in mind and whether he wanted to hurt me. I tried to decide whether if I screamed now, screamed loud and piercingly, someone could come down from above quickly enough to save me. But I gave up the idea.

"What is it?" I asked. "What do you want?"

"Nothing much. I only wanted to ask you something. The others don't have to hear it."

"Oh, really? I can't think of anything to say to you. I have to go up, you know."

Softly Franz Kromer asked: "You know who owns the orchard by the mill, don't you?"

"I'm not sure. The miller, I think."

Franz had put his arm around me and now he drew me so close I was forced to look into his face inches away. His eyes were evil, he smiled maliciously; his face was filled with cruelty and a sense of power.

"Well, I can tell you for certain whose orchard that is. I've known for some time that someone had stolen apples there and that the man who owns it said he'd give two marks to anyone who'd tell him who swiped them."

"Oh, my God!" I exclaimed. "You wouldn't do that, would you?"

I felt it would be useless to appeal to his sense of honor. He came from the other world: betrayal was no crime to him. I sensed this acutely. The people from the other world were not like us in these matters.

"Not say anything?" laughed Kromer. "Kid, what do you take me for? Do you think I own a mint? I'm poor, I don't have a wealthy father like you and if I can earn two marks I earn them any way I can. Maybe he'll even give me more."

Suddenly he let go of me. The passageway no longer smelled of peace and safety, the world around me began to crumble. He would give me away to the police! I was a criminal; my father would be informed—perhaps even the police would come. All the dread of chaos threatened me, everything ugly and dangerous was united against me. It meant nothing that I'd filched nothing. I'd sworn I had!

Tears welled up in my eyes. I felt I had to strike a bargain and desperately I groped through all my pockets. Not a single apple, no pocket knife, I had nothing at all. I thought of my watch, an old silver watch that didn't work, that I wore just for the fun of it. It had been my grandmother's. Quickly I took it off.

I said: "Kromer, listen! Don't give me away. It wouldn't be fair if you did. I'll give you my watch as a present, here, take a look. Otherwise I've nothing at all. You can have it, it's made of silver, and the works, well, there's something slightly wrong with them; you have to have it fixed."

He smiled and weighed the watch in his palm. I looked at his hand and felt how brutal and deeply hostile it was to me, how it reached for my life and peace.

"It's made of silver," I said hesitantly.

"I don't give a damn for your silver and your old watch," he said scornfully. "Get it fixed yourself."

"But, Franz!" I exclaimed, trembling with fear that he

might run away. "Wait, wait a moment. Why don't you take it? It's really made of silver, honest. And I don't have anything else."

He threw me a cold scornful look.

"Well, you know who I'll go to. Or I could go to the police too. . . . I'm on good terms with the sergeant."

He turned as if to go. I held on to his sleeve. I couldn't allow him to go. I would rather have died than suffer what might happen if he went off like that.

"Franz," I implored, hoarse with excitement, "don't do anything foolish. You're only joking, aren't you?"

"Yes, I'm joking, but it could turn into an expensive joke."

"Just tell me what I'm supposed to do, Franz. I'll do anything you ask."

He looked me up and down with narrowed eyes and laughed again.

"Don't be so stupid," he said with false good humor. "You know as well as I that I'm in a position to earn two marks. I'm not a rich man who can afford to throw them away, but you're rich—you even have a watch. All you have to do is give me two marks; then everything will be all right."

I understood his logic. But two marks! That was as much and as unattainable as ten, as a hundred, as a thousand. I didn't have a pfennig. There was a piggy bank that my mother kept for me. When relatives came to visit they would drop in five- or ten-pfennig pieces. That was all I had. I had no allowance at that time.

"I just don't have any," I said sadly. "I don't have any money at all. But I'll give you everything else I have. I have a Western, tin soldiers, and a compass. Wait, I'll get them for you."

Kromer's mouth merely twisted into a brief sneer. Then he spit on the floor.

Harshly he said: "You can keep your crap. A compass! Don't make me mad! You hear, I'm after money."

"But I don't have any, I never get any, I can't help it."

"All right, then you'll bring me the two marks tomorrow. I'll wait for you after school down near the market place. That's all. You'll see what'll happen if you don't bring it."

"But where am I going to get it if I don't have any?"

"There's plenty of money in your house. That's your business. Tomorrow after school. And I'm telling you: if you don't have it with you . . ." He threw me a withering look, spit once more, and vanished like a shadow.

I couldn't even get upstairs. My life was wrecked. I thought of running away and never coming back, or of drowning myself. However, I couldn't picture any of this very clearly. In the dark, I sat down on the bottom step of our staircase, huddled up within myself, abandoning myself to misery. That's where Lina found me weeping as she came downstairs with the basket to fetch wood.

I begged her not to say a word, then I went upstairs. To the right of the glass door hung my father's hat and my mother's parasol; they gave me a feeling of home and comfort, and my heart greeted them thankfully, as the Prodigal Son might greet the sight and smell of old familiar rooms. But all of it was lost to me now, all of it belonged to the clear, well-lighted world of my father and mother, and I, guilty and deeply engulfed in an alien world, was entangled in adventures and sin, threatened by an enemy, —by dangers, fear, and shame. The hat and parasol, the old sandstone floor I was so fond of, the broad picture above the hall cupboard, the voice of my elder sister coming to me from the living room were all more moving, more precious, more delicious than ever before, but they had ceased to be a refuge and something I could rely on; they had become an unmistakable reproach. None of this was mine any more, I could no longer take part in its quiet cheerfulness. My feet had become muddied, I could not even wipe them clean on the mat; everywhere I went I was followed by a darkness of which this world of home knew nothing. How many secrets I had had, how often I had been afraid—but all of it had been child's play compared with what I brought home with me today. I was haunted by misfortune, it was reaching out toward me so that not even my mother could protect me, since she was not even allowed to know. Whether my crime was stealing or lying—(hadn't I sworn a false oath by God and everything that was sacred?)—was immaterial. My sin was not specifically this or that but consisted of having shaken hands with the devil. Why had I gone along? Why had I obeyed Kromer—better even than I had ever obeyed my father? Why had I invented the story, building myself up with a crime as though it were a heroic act? The devil held me in his clutches, the enemy was behind me.

For the time being I was not so much afraid of what would happen tomorrow as of the horrible certainty that my way, from now on, would lead farther and farther downhill into darkness. I felt acutely that new offenses were bound to grow out of this one offense, that my presence among my sisters, greeting and kissing my parents, were a lie, that I was living a lie concealed deep inside myself.

For a moment, hope and confidence flickered up inside me as I gazed at my father's hat. I would tell him everything, would accept his verdict and his punishment, and would make him into my confessor and savior. It would only be a penance, the kind I had often done, a bitterly difficult hour, a ruefully difficult request for forgiveness.

How sweet and tempting that sounded! But it was no use. I knew I wouldn't do it. I knew I now had a secret, a sin which I would have to expiate alone. Perhaps I stood at the parting of the ways, perhaps I would now belong among the wicked forever, share their secrets, depend on them, obey them, have to become one of their kind. I had acted the man and hero, now I had to bear the consequences.

I was glad when my father took me to task for my muddy boots. It diverted his attention by sidestepping the real issue and placed me in a position to endure reproaches that I could secretly transfer to the other, the more serious offense. A strange new feeling overcame me at this point, a feeling that stung pleasurably: I felt superior to my father! Momentarily I felt a certain loathing for his ignorance. His upbraiding me for muddy boots seemed pitiful. "If you only knew" crossed my mind as I stood there like a criminal being cross-examined for a stolen loaf of bread when the actual crime was murder. It was an odious, hostile feeling, but it was strong and deeply attractive, and shackled me more than anything else to my secret and my guilt. I thought Kromer might have gone to the police by now and denounced me, that thunderstorms were forming above my head, while all this time they continued to treat me like a little child.

This moment was the most significant and lasting of the whole experience. It was the first rent in the holy image of my father, it was the first fissure in the columns that had upheld my childhood, which every individual must destroy before he can become himself. The inner, the essential line of our fate consists of such invisible experiences. Such fissures and rents grow together again, heal and are forgotten, but in the most secret recesses they continue to live and bleed.

I immediately felt such dread of this new feeling that I could have fallen down before my father and kissed his feet to ask forgiveness. But one cannot apologize for something fundamental, and a child feels and knows this as well and as deeply as any sage.

I felt the need to give some thought to my new situation, to reflect about what I would do tomorrow. But I did not find the time. All evening I was busy getting used to the changed atmosphere in our living room. Wall clock and table, Bible and mirror, bookcase and pictures on the wall were leaving me behind; I was forced to observe with a chill in my heart how my world, my good, happy, carefree life, was becoming a part of the past, was breaking away from me, and I was forced to feel how I was being shackled and held fast with new roots to the outside, to the dark and alien world. For the first time in my life I tasted death, and death tasted bitter, for death is birth, is fear and dread of some terrible renewal.

I was glad when I finally lay in my bed. Just before, as my last torment, I had had to endure evening prayers. We had sung a hymn which was one of my favorites. I felt unable to join in and every note galled me. When my father intoned the blessing—when he finished with "God be with us!"—something broke inside me and I was rejected forever from this intimate circle. God's grace was with all of them, but it was no longer with me. Cold and deeply exhausted, I had left them.

When I had lain in bed awhile, enveloped by its warmth and safety, my fearful heart turned back once more in confusion and hovered anxiously above what was now past. My mother had said good night to me as always. I could still hear her steps resound in the other room; the candle glow still illuminated the chink in the door. Now, I thought, now she'll come back once more, she has sensed something, she will give me a kiss and ask, ask kindly with a promise in her voice, and then I'll weep, then the lump in my throat will melt, then I will throw my arms around her, and then all will be well; I will be saved! And even after the chink in the door had gone dark I continued to listen and was certain that it simply would have to happen.

Then I returned to my difficulties and looked my enemy in the eye. I could see him clearly, one eye screwed up, his mouth twisted into a brutal smile, and while I eyed him, becoming more and more convinced of the inevitable, he grew bigger and uglier and his evil eye lit up with a fiendish glint. He was right next to me until I fell asleep, yet I didn't dream of him nor of what had happened that day. I dreamed instead that my parents, my sisters, and I were drifting in a boat, surrounded by absolute peace and the glow of a holiday. In the middle of the night I woke with the aftertaste of this happiness. I could still see my sisters' white summer dresses shimmer in the sun as I fell out of paradise back into reality, again face to face with the enemy, with his evil eye.

Next morning, when my mother came rushing up shouting that it was late and why was I still in bed, I looked sick. When she asked me whether anything was wrong, I vomited.

This seemed to be something gained. I loved being slightly sick, being allowed to lie in bed all morning, drinking camomile tea, listening to my mother tidy up the other rooms or Lina deal with the butcher in the hallway. Mornings off from school seemed enchanted, like a fairy tale; the sun playing in the room was not the same sun shut out of school when the green shades were lowered. Yet even this gave me no pleasure today; there was something false about it.

If only I could die! But, as often before, I was only slightly unwell and it was of no help, my illness protected me from school but not from Franz Kromer who would be waiting for me at eleven in the market place. And my mother's friendliness, instead of comforting me, was a distressing nuisance. I made a show of having fallen asleep again in order to be left alone to think. But I could see no way out. At eleven I had to be at the market. At ten I quietly got dressed and said that I felt better. The answer, as usual under these circumstances, was: either I went straight back to bed or in the afternoon I would have to be in school. I said I would gladly go to school. I had come up with a plan.

I couldn't meet Kromer penniless. I had to get hold of my piggy bank. I knew it didn't contain enough, by no means enough, yet it was something, and I sensed that something was better than nothing, and that Kromer could at least be appeased.

In stocking feet I crept guiltily into my mother's room and took the piggy bank out of her desk; yet that was not half as bad as what had happened the day before with Kromer. My heart beat so rapidly I felt I would choke. It did not ease up when I discovered downstairs that the bank was locked. Forcing it was easy, it was merely a matter of tearing the thin tin-plate grid; yet breaking it hurt—only now had I really committed a theft. Until then I had filched lumps of sugar or some fruit; this was more serious stealing, even though it was my own money I stole. I sensed how I was one step nearer Kromer and his world, how bit by bit everything was going downhill with me. I began to feel stubborn; let the devil take the hindmost! There was no turning back now. Nervously I counted the money. In the piggy bank it had sounded like so much more, but there was painfully little lying in my hand: sixty-five pfennigs. I hid the box on the ground floor, held the money clasped in my fist, and stepped out of the house, feeling more different than I had ever felt before when I walked through the gate. I thought I heard someone calling after me from upstairs but I walked away quickly.

There was still a lot of time left. By a very devious route, I sneaked through the little alleys of a changed town, under a cloudy sky such as I had never seen before, past staring houses and people who eyed me with suspicion. Then it occurred to me that a friend from school had once found a thaler in the cattle market. I would gladly have gone down on my knees and prayed that God perform a miracle and let me make a similar find. But I had forfeited the right to pray. And in any case, mending the box would have required a second miracle.

Franz Kromer spotted me from a distance, yet he approached me without haste and seemed to ignore me. When he was close, he motioned authoritatively for me to follow him, and without once turning back he walked calmly down the Strohgasse and across the little foot-bridge until he stopped in front of a new building at the outskirts. There were no workmen about, the walls were bare, doors and windows were blanks. Kromer took a look around, then walked through the entrance into the house and I followed him. He stepped behind a wall, gave me a signal, and stretched out his hand.

"Have you got it?" he asked coolly.

I drew my clenched fist out of my pocket and emptied my money into his flat outstretched palm. He had counted it even before the last pfennig piece had clinked down.

"That's sixty-five pfennigs," he said and looked at me.

"Yes," I said nervously. "That's all I have. I know it's not enough, but it's all I have."

"I thought you were cleverer than that," he scolded almost mildly. "Among men of honor you've got to do things right. I don't want to take anything away from you that isn't the right sum. You know that. Take your pennies back, there! The other one—you know who—won't try to scale down the price. He pays up."

"But I simply don't have another pfennig. It's all I had in my bank."

"That's your business. But I don't want to make you unhappy. You owe me one mark, thirty-five pfennigs. When can I have them?"

"Oh, you'll get them for sure, Kromer. I just don't know when right now—perhaps I'll have more tomorrow or the day after. You understand, don't you, that I can't breathe a word about this to my father."

"That's not my concern. I'm not out to do you any harm. I could have my money before lunch if I wanted, you know, and I'm poor. You wear expensive clothes and you're better fed than I. But I won't say anything. I can wait a bit. The day after tomorrow I'll whistle for you. You know what my whistle sounds like, don't you?"

He let me hear it. I had heard it before.

"Yes," I said, "I know it."

He left me as though he'd never seen me before. It had been a business transaction between the two of us, nothing more.

I think Kromer's whistle would frighten me even today if I suddenly heard it again. From now on I was to hear it repeatedly; it seemed to me I heard it all the time. There was not a single place, not a single game, no activity, no thought which this whistle did not penetrate, the whistle that made me his slave, that had become my fate. Frequently I would go into our small flower garden, of which I was so fond on those mild, colorful autumn afternoons, and an odd urge prompted me to play once more the childish games of my earlier years; I was playing, so to speak, the part of someone younger than myself, someone still good and free, innocent and safe. Yet into the midst of this haven—always expected, yet horribly surprising each time—from somewhere Kromer's whistle would erupt, destroying the game, crushing my illusions. Then I would have to leave the garden to follow my tormentor to wicked, ugly places where I would have to give him an account of my pitiful finances and let myself be pressed for payment. The entire episode lasted perhaps several weeks, yet to me they seemed like years, an eternity.

Rarely did I have any money, at most a five- or ten-pfennig piece stolen from the kitchen table when Lina had left the shopping basket lying around. Kromer upbraided me each time, becoming more and more contemptuous: I was cheating him, depriving him of what was rightfully his, I was stealing from him, making *him* miserable! Never in my life had I felt so distressed, never had I felt more hopeless, more enslaved.

I had filled the piggy bank with play money and replaced it in my mother's desk. No one asked for it but the possibility that they might never left my thoughts. What frightened me even more than Kromer's brutal whistling was my mother's stepping up to me—wasn't she coming to inquire about the piggy bank?

Because I had met my tormentor many times empty-handed, he began finding other means of torturing and using me. I had to work for him. He had to run various errands for his father; I had to do them for him. Or he would ask me to perform some difficult feat: hop for ten minutes on one leg, pin a scrap of paper on a passer-by's coat. Many nights in my dreams I elaborated on these tortures and lay drenched in a nightmare's sweat.

For a while I actually became sick. I vomited frequently and came down with frequent chills, yet at night I would burn and sweat. My mother sensed that something was wrong and was very considerate, but this only tortured me the more since I could not respond by confiding in her.

One night, after I had gone to bed, she brought me a piece of chocolate. It reminded me of former years when, if I had been a good boy, I would receive such rewards before I fell asleep. Now she stood there and offered me the piece of chocolate. The sight was so painful that I could only shake my head. She asked me what was wrong and stroked my hair. All I could answer was: "No, no! I don't want anything." She placed the chocolate on my night table and left. The next morning, when she wanted to ask me about my behavior of the night before, I pretended to have forgotten the episode completely. Once she brought the doctor, who examined me and prescribed cold baths in the morning.

My condition at that time was a kind of madness. Amid the ordered peace of our house I lived shyly, in agony, like a ghost; I took no part in the life of the others, rarely forgot myself for an hour at a time. To my father, who was often irritated and asked me what was the matter, I was completely cold.

2)   Cain

MY SALVATION CAME from a totally unexpected source, which, at the same time, brought a new element into my life that has affected it to this very day.

A new boy had just been enrolled in our school. He was the son of a well-to-do widow who had come to live in our town; he wore a mourning band on his sleeve. Being several years older than I, he was assigned to a grade above me. Still, I could not avoid noticing him, nor could anyone else. This remarkable student seemed much older than he looked; in fact, he did not strike anyone as a boy at all. In contrast to us, he seemed strange and mature, like a man, or rather like a gentleman. He was not popular, did not take part in our games, still less in the general roughhouse, and only his firm, self-confident tone toward the teachers won the admiration of the students. He was called Max Demian.

One day—as happened now and again—an additional class was assigned to our large classroom for some reason or other. It was Demian's class. We, the younger ones,

were having a Scripture lesson; the higher grade had to
write an essay. While the story of Cain and Abel was
being drummed into us, I kept glancing toward Demian
whose face held a peculiar fascination for me, and I ob-
served the intelligent, light, unusually resolute face bent
attentively and diligently over his work; he didn't at all
look like a student doing an assignment, but rather like a
scientist investigating a problem of his own. I couldn't say
that he made a favorable impression on me; on the contrary, I had something against him: he seemed too superior
and detached, his manner too provocatively confident,
and his eyes gave him an adult expression—which
children never like—faintly sad, with flashes of sarcasm.
Yet I could not help looking at him, no matter whether I
liked or detested him, but if he happened to glance my
way I averted my eyes in panic. When I think back on it
today, and what he looked like as a student at that time, I
can only say that he was in every respect different from all
the others, was entirely himself, with a personality all his
own which made him noticeable even though he did his
best not to be noticed; his manner and bearing was that of
a prince disguised among farm boys, taking great pains to
appear one of them.

He was walking behind me on the way home from
school, and after the others had turned off he caught up
with me and said hello. Even his manner of greeting,
though he tried to imitate our schoolboy tone, was distinctly adult and polite.

"Shall we walk together for a while?" he asked. I felt
flattered and nodded. Then I described to him where I
lived.

"Oh, over there?" he said and smiled. "I know the

house. There's something odd above the doorway—it interested me at once."

I didn't know offhand what he meant and was astonished that he apparently knew our house better than I did myself. The keystone of the arch above the doorway bore no doubt a kind of coat of arms but it had worn off with time and had frequently been painted over. As far as I knew it had nothing to do with us and our family.

"I don't know anything about it," I said shyly. "It's a bird or something like that and must be quite old. The house is supposed to have been part of the monastery at one point."

"That's quite possible." He nodded. "Take a good look at it sometime! Such things can be quite interesting. I believe it's a sparrow hawk."

We walked on. I felt very self-conscious. Suddenly Demian laughed as though something had struck him as funny.

"Yes, when we had class together," he burst out. "The story of Cain who has that mark on his forehead. Do you like it?"

No, I didn't. It was rare for me to like anything we had to learn. Yet I didn't dare confess it, for I felt I was being addressed by an adult. I said I didn't much mind the story.

Demian slapped me on the back.

"You don't have to put on an act for me. But in fact the story is quite remarkable. It's far more remarkable than most stories we're taught in school. Your teacher didn't go into it at great length. He just mentioned the usual things about God and sin and so forth. But I believe—" He interrupted himself and asked with a smile: "Does this interest you at all?"

"Well, I think," he went on, "one can give this story about Cain quite a different interpretation. Most of the things we're taught I'm sure are quite right and true, but one can view all of them from quite a different angle than the teachers do—and most of the time they then make better sense. For instance, one can't be quite satisfied with this Cain and the mark on his forehead, with the way it's explained to us. Don't you agree? It's perfectly possible for someone to kill his brother with a stone and to panic and repent. But that he's awarded a special decoration for his cowardice, a mark that protects him and puts the fear of God into all the others, that's quite odd, isn't it?"

"Of course," I said with interest: the idea began to fascinate me. "But what other way of interpreting the story is there?"

He slapped me on the shoulder.

"It's quite simple! The first element of the story, its actual beginning, was the mark. Here was a man with something in his face that frightened the others. They didn't dare lay hands on him; he impressed them, he and his children. We can guess—no, we can be quite certain—that it was not a mark on his forehead like a postmark—life is hardly ever as clear and straightforward as that. It is much more likely that he struck people as faintly sinister, perhaps a little more intellect and boldness in his look than people were used to. This man was powerful: you would approach him only with awe. He had a 'sign.' You could explain this any way you wished. And people always want what is agreeable to them and puts them in the right. They were afraid of Cain's children: they bore a 'sign.' So they did not interpret the sign for what it was — a mark of distinction—but as its opposite. They said: 'Those fellows with the sign, they're a strange lot'—and indeed they were. People with courage and character always seem sinister to the rest. It was a scandal that a breed of fearless and sinister people ran about freely, so they attached a nickname and myth to these people to get even with them, to make up for the many times they had felt afraid—do you get it?"

"Yes—that is—in that case Cain wouldn't have been evil at all? And the whole story in the Bible is actually not authentic?"

"Yes and no. Such age-old stories are always true but they aren't always properly recorded and aren't always given correct interpretations. In short, I mean Cain was a fine fellow and this story was pinned on him only because people were afraid. The story was simply a rumor, something that people gab about, and it was true in so far as Cain and his children really bore a kind of mark and were different from most people."

I was astounded.

"And do you believe that the business about killing his brother isn't true either?" I asked, entranced.

"Oh, that's certainly true. The strong man slew a weaker one. It's doubtful whether it was really his brother. But it isn't important. Ultimately all men are brothers. So, a strong man slew a weaker one: perhaps it was a truly valiant act, perhaps it wasn't. At any rate, all the other weaker ones were afraid of him from then on, they complained bitterly and if you asked them: 'Why don't you turn around and slay him, too?' they did not reply 'Because we're cowards,' but rather 'You can't, he has a sign. God has marked him.' The fraud must have originated some way like that.—Oh well, I see I'm keeping you. So long then."

He turned into the Altgasse and left me standing there, more baffled than I had ever been in my life. Yet, almost as soon as he had gone, everything he had said seemed incredible. Cain a noble person, Abel a coward! Cain's mark a mark of distinction! It was absurd, it was blasphemous and evil. How did God fit in in that case? Hadn't He accepted the sacrifice of Abel? Didn't He love Abel? No, what Demian had said was completely crazy. And I suspected that he had wanted to make fun of me and make me lose my footing. He was clever all right, and he could talk, but he couldn't put that one over, not on me!

I had never before given as much thought to a biblical story or to any other story. And for a long time I had not forgotten Franz Kromer as completely; for hours, for a whole evening in fact. At home I read the story once more as written in the Bible. It was brief and unambiguous; it was quite mad to look for a special, hidden meaning. At that rate every murderer could declare that he was God's darling! No, what Demian had said was nonsense. What pleased me was the ease and grace with which he was able to say such things, as though everything were self-evident; and then the look in his eyes!

Something was very wrong with me, though; my life was in very great disorder. I had lived in a wholesome and clean world, had been a kind of Abel myself, and now I was stuck deeply in the "other world," had fallen and sunk very low—yet it hadn't basically been my fault! How was I to consider that? And now a memory flashed within me that for a moment almost left me breathless. On that fatal evening when my misery had begun, there had been that matter with my father. There, for a moment, I had seen through him and his world of light and wisdom and had felt nothing but contempt for it. Yes, at that moment I, who was Cain and bore the mark, had imagined that this sign was not a mark of shame and that because of my evil and misfortune I stood higher than my father and the pious, the righteous.

I had not experienced the moment in this form, in clearly expressed thoughts, but all of this had been contained within it; it had been the eruption of emotions, of strange stirrings, that hurt me yet filled me with pride at the same time.

When I considered how strangely Demian had talked about the fearless and the cowardly, what an unusual meaning he had given the mark Cain bore on his forehead, how his eyes, his remarkable adult eyes had lit up, the question flashed through my mind whether Demian himself was not a kind of Cain. Why does he defend Cain unless he feels an affinity with him? Why does he have such a powerful gaze? Why does he speak so contemptuously of the "others," of the timid who actually are the pious, the chosen ones of the Lord?

I could not bring these thoughts to any conclusion. A stone had been dropped into the well, the well was my youthful soul. And for a very long time this matter of Cain, the fratricide, and the "mark" formed the point of departure for all my attempts at comprehension, my doubts and my criticism.

I noticed that Demian exerted equal fascination over the other students. I hadn't told anyone about his version of the story of Cain, but the others seemed to be interested in him, too. At any rate, many rumors were in circulation about the "new boy." If I could only remember them all now, each one would throw some light on him and could be intepreted. I remember first that Demian's mother was reported to be wealthy and also, supposedly, neither she nor her son ever attended church. One story had it that they were Jewish but they might equally well have been secret Mohammedans. Then there was Max Demian's legendary physical prowess. But this could be corroborated: when the strongest boy in Demian's class had taunted him, calling him a coward when he refused to fight back, Demian had humiliated him. Those who were present told that Demian had grasped the boy with one hand by the neck and squeezed until the boy went pale; afterwards, the boy had slunk away and had not been able to use his arm for a whole week. One evening some boys even claimed that he was dead. For a time everything, even the most extravagant assertions were believed. Then everyone seemed to have had their fill of Demian for a while, though not much later gossip again flourished: some boys reported that Demian was intimate with girls and that he "knew everything."

Meanwhile, my business with Kromer took its inevitable course. I couldn't escape him, for even when he left me alone for days I was still bound to him. He haunted my dreams and what he failed to perpetrate on me in real life, my imagination let him do to me in those dreams in which I was completely his slave. I have always been a great dreamer; in dreams I am more active than in my real life, and these shadows sapped me of health and energy. A recurring nightmare was that Kromer always maltreated me, spit and knelt on me and, what was worse, led me on to commit the most horrible crimes—or, rather, not so much led me on as compelled me through sheer force of persuasion. The worst of these dreams, from which I awoke half-mad, had to do with a murderous assault on my father. Kromer whetted a knife, put it in my hand; we stood behind some trees in an avenue and lay in wait for someone, I did not know whom. Yet when this someone approached and Kromer pinched my arm to let me know that this was the person I was to stab—it was my father. Then I would awake.

Although I still drew a connection between these events and the story of Cain and Abel, I gave little thought to Max Demian. When he first approached me again, it was, oddly enough, also in a dream. For I was still dreaming of being tortured. Yet this time it was Demian who knelt on me. And—this was totally new and left a deep impression on me—everything I had resisted and that had been agony to me when Kromer was my tormentor I suffered gladly at Demian's hands, with a feeling compounded as much of ecstasy as of fear. I had this dream twice. Then Kromer regained his old place.

For years I have been unable to distinguish between what I experienced in these dreams and in real life. In any event, the bad relationship with Kromer continued and by no means came to an end after I had finally paid my debt out of any number of petty thefts. No, for now he knew of these new thefts since he asked each time where I had gotten the money, and I was more in bondage to him than ever. Often he threatened to tell everything to my father but even then my fear was hardly as great as my profound regret at not having done so myself at the very beginning. In the meantime, miserable though I was, I did not regret everything that happened, at least not all the time, and occasionally I even felt that everything had had to happen as it did. I was in the hands of fate and it was useless to try to escape.

Presumably, my parents also were distressed by the state I was in. A strange spirit had taken hold of me, I no longer fitted into our community, once so intimate; yet often a wild longing came over me to return to it as to a lost paradise. My mother in particular treated me more like an invalid than a scoundrel, but my true status within the family I was better able to judge from my sisters' attitude. Theirs was one of extreme indulgence, which made it plain that I was considered a kind of madman, more to be pitied for his condition than blamed, but possessed by the devil nonetheless. They prayed for me with unusual fervor and I was infinitely miserable when I realized the futility of these prayers. Often I felt a burning need for relief, for genuine confession, and yet sensed in advance that I would be unable to tell my mother or father, and explain everything properly. I knew that everything I said would be accepted sympathetically, that they would, yes, even feel sorry for me, but that they would not understand, that the whole thing would be regarded as a momentary aberration, whereas in truth it was my fate.

I realize that some people will not believe that a child of little more than ten years is capable of having such feelings. My story is not intended for them. I am telling it to those who have a better knowledge of man. The adult who has learned to translate a part of his feelings into thoughts notices the absence of these thoughts in a child, and therefore comes to believe that the child lacks these experiences, too. Yet rarely in my life have I felt and suffered as deeply as at that time.

One day it rained. Kromer had ordered me to meet him at the Burgplatz, and there I stood and waited, shuffling among the wet chestnut leaves that were still falling from the black wet trees. I had no money with me but I had managed to put aside two pieces of cake and had brought them along so as to be able to give Kromer something at least. By now I was used to standing in some corner and waiting for him, often for a very long time, and I accepted it the same way one learns to put up with the inevitable.

Kromer showed up finally. He didn't stay long. He poked me in the ribs a few times, laughed, took the cake, even offered me a damp cigarette (which, however, I did not accept), and was friendlier than usual.

"Yes," he said nonchalantly before going away, "before I forget it, you might bring your sister along the next time, the older one, what's her name."

I failed to get his point and made no reply. I only looked at him, surprised.

"Don't you understand? You're to bring your sister."

"No, Kromer, that's impossible. I wouldn't be allowed to and she wouldn't come in any case."

I was prepared for this new ruse or pretext of his. He did this often: demanded something impossible, frightened and humiliated me, then gradually offered some bargain as a way out, and I had to buy myself off with some money or a gift.

This time, however, it was altogether different. My refusal did not seem to make him angry at all.

"Well, anyway," he said in a matter-of-fact tone, "think it over. I'd like to meet your sister. We'll find a way one of these days. You could simply take her along on a walk and then I could join you. I'll give you a whistle tomorrow, then we can talk about it some more."

After he had left, something of the nature of his request suddenly dawned on me. I was still quite ignorant in these matters but I knew from hearsay that boys and girls when they grew older were able to do certain mysterious, repulsive, forbidden things together. And now I was supposed to—it suddenly flashed on me how monstrous his request was! I knew at once that I would never do it. But what would happen then? What revenge would Kromer take on me? I didn't dare think of it. This was the beginning of a new torture for me.

Inconsolable, I walked across the desolate square, hands in my pockets. Further and greater agonies awaited me!

Suddenly a vigorous cheerful voice called me. I was startled and began to flee. Someone ran after me, a hand grasped me gently from behind. It was Max Demian.

"Oh, it's you," I said mistrustfully. "You gave me a terrible shock."

He looked down at me and never had his look been more adult, superior, the look of someone who could see through me. We had not spoken to each other for a long time.

"I feel sorry for you," he said in his polite yet decisive manner. "Listen, you can't let yourself be frightened like that."

"Well, one can't always help it."

"So it seems. But look: if you practically go to pieces in front of someone who hasn't done you any harm, then that someone begins to think. He's surprised, he becomes inquisitive, he thinks you're remarkably high-strung and reaches the conclusion that people are always like that when they're deathly afraid. Cowards are constantly afraid, but you're not a coward, are you? Certainly, you're no hero either. There are some things you're afraid of, and some people, too. And that should never be, you should never be afraid of men. You aren't afraid of me? Or are you?"

"Oh, no, not at all."

"Exactly. But there are people you are frightened of?"

"I don't know. . . . Why don't you let me be?"

He kept pace with me—I had quickened my steps with thoughts of escaping—and I felt him glancing at me from the side.

"Let's assume," he began again, "that I don't mean to do you any harm. At any rate, you've no need to be afraid of me. I'd like to try out an experiment on you. It might be fun and you might even learn something from it. Now pay attention!—You see, I sometimes practice an art known as thought reading. There's no black magic about it but if you don't know how it's done it can seem very uncanny. You can shock people with it, too. Now let's give it a try. Well, I like you, or I'm interested in you and would like to discover what goes on inside you. I've already taken the initial step in that direction: I've frightened you—so that you're nervous. There must be things and people that you're afraid of. If you are afraid of someone, the most likely reason is that this someone has something on you. For example, you've done something wrong and the other person knows it—he has a hold on you. You get it? Very clear, isn't it?"

I looked up helplessly at his face, which was as serious and intelligent as ever, and kind. Yet its detached severity lacked tenderness; impartiality or something similar was visible in it. I was hardly aware of what was happening to me: he stood before me like a magician.

"Have you got it?" he asked once more.

I nodded, unable to speak.

"I told you, reading other people's thoughts seems strange but it's perfectly natural. For instance, I could tell you almost exactly what you thought about me the time I told you the story of Cain and Abel. Well, this isn't the time to talk of that. I also think it possible that you dreamed about me once. But let's put that aside, too. You're bright and most people are stupid. I like talking to a bright fellow now and then, someone I can trust. You don't mind, do you?"

"Of course not. But I don't understand . . ."

"Let's keep to our amusing experiment for the moment. So, we've discovered that boy S is easily frightened—he's afraid of someone—he probably shares a secret with this other person, a secret that makes him feel uneasy. Roughly speaking, does this correspond to the facts?"

As though in a dream, I succumbed to his voice and influence. His voice seemed to come from within myself. And it knew everything. Did it know everything more clearly and better than I did myself?

Demian slapped me firmly on the shoulder.

"So that's what it is. I thought it might be. Now just one more question: do you happen to know the name of the boy who left you back there at the Burgplatz?"

I was terrified. He had touched my secret.

"What boy? There wasn't any boy there, only me."

"Go on." He laughed. "What's his name?"

"Do you mean Franz Kromer?" I whispered.

He gave me a satisfied nod.

"Excellent. You're all right, we'll become friends yet. But first I have to tell you something: this Kromer, or whatever his name is, his face tells me he's a first-rate bastard. What do you think?"

"Yes," I sighed, "he's pretty bad. But he mustn't hear about this. For God's sake. He mustn't find out anything. Do you know him? Does he know you?"

"Relax. He's gone and he doesn't know me—not yet. But I'd like to meet him. He goes to public school, doesn't he?"

"Yes."

"What grade's he in?"

"The fifth. But don't say anything to him. Please."

"Don't worry, nothing will happen to you. I take it you don't want to tell me more about this Kromer?"

"I can't."

He was silent for a while.

"Too bad," he said. "We could have carried the experiment a stage further. But I don't want to get you all upset. However, you realize, don't you, that your fear of him is all wrong? Such fear can destroy us completely. You've got to get rid of it, you've simply got to, if you want to turn into someone decent. You understand that, don't you?"

"Certainly, you're completely right. . . . But it's so complicated. . . . You've no idea . . ."

"You've seen that I know quite a few things about you, far more than you would have imagined.—Do you owe him any money?"

"Yes, that too. But that's not the main thing. I can't tell you, I just can't."

"Wouldn't it help if I gave you as much as you owe him?"

"No, that's not it. And you promise not to tell anyone about it? Not a word?"

"You can trust me, Sinclair. You can tell me your secret some other time."

"Never!" I shouted.

"As you like. All I meant was: perhaps you'll tell me more some other time. Voluntarily, of course. You don't think I would treat you the way Kromer does, do you?"

"Oh, no—but what do you know about that anyhow?"

"Nothing whatever. I've merely thought it over and I'd never do it Kromer's way, you can believe that. Besides, you don't owe me anything."

We did not speak for a long time, and I began to calm down, yet I found Demian's knowledge all the more puzzling.

"I'm going home now," he said and gathered his coat closer around him in the rain. "There's just one more thing I'd like to say to you since we've gotten so far—you ought to get rid of this bastard! If there's no other way of doing it, kill him. It would impress and please me if you did! I'd even lend you a hand."

The story of Cain suddenly recurred to me, and I became afraid again. Everything began to seem so ominous to me that I began to whimper. I was surrounded by too much that I didn't understand.

"All right." Max Demian smiled. "Go on home. We'll find a way, even though killing him would be the simplest. In cases like this, the simplest course is always the best. Your friend Kromer isn't the best friend to have."

I found my way home and it seemed to me that I had

been away for a year. Everything looked different. Something like a future, like hope, now separated me from Kromer. I was no longer alone. Only now did I realize how horribly alone I had been with my secret for weeks on end. And at once I remembered a thought I had had several times before: that a confession to my parents would lighten my load but would not entirely relieve me of it. Now I had almost confessed, to another, to a stranger, and the sense of relief was like a fresh breeze.

Nonetheless, my fear was far from conquered and I was prepared for a long series of terrible wrangles with my enemy. That was why it seemed remarkable that matters took such a calm, such a discreet course.

For one day, for two, for a whole week there was no sound of Kromer's whistle near our house. I hardly dared believe it and I constantly lay in wait for the moment when suddenly, when least expected, he would reappear. He seemed to have vanished. Mistrusting my new freedom, I refused to believe in it, that is, until I finally ran into Franz Kromer. When he saw me he flinched, his face twitched, and he turned away so as to avoid meeting me.

It was an unprecedented moment for me! My enemy fleeing from me, my devil afraid of me! A thrill of happy surprise overwhelmed me.

One day I ran into Demian again. He was waiting for me in front of school.

"Hello," I said.

"Good morning, Sinclair. I only wanted to hear how things were going. Kromer isn't bothering you any more, is he?"

"Is that your doing? How did you manage it? I don't understand it at all. He's staying away altogether."

"That's good. If he should turn up again—I don't think he will, but he's quite ruthless—just tell him not to forget Max Demian."

"But what's the connection? Did you pick a fight and beat him up?"

"No, that's not my way of doing things. I merely talked to him as I did to you and was able to make it clear to him that it is to his advantage to leave you alone."

"You didn't pay him any money, I hope."

"No, that's your method."

He evaded all my questions, leaving me with the same uneasy feeling toward him I'd had before: a strange mixture of gratitude and awe, admiration and fear, sympathy and inward resistance.

I decided to seek him out and talk at length about all these matters, as well as about the Cain business.

But it did not happen that way.

Gratitude is not a virtue I believe in, and to me it seems hypocritical to expect it from a child. Thus my total ingratitude toward Max Demian does not astonish me too much. Today I have no doubt whatever that I would have been sick and ruined for life had he not freed me from Kromer's clutches. Even at that time I was conscious that this liberation was the greatest experience of my life—but the liberator himself I deserted as soon as he had performed his miracle.

As I have said, ingratitude does not surprise me. What does startle me, in retrospect, is my lack of curiosity. How was I able to go on living a single day without trying to come nearer to the secret which Demian had revealed to me? How was it I did not want to hear more about Cain, more about Kromer, more about Demian's ability to read other people's thoughts?

It is almost incredible, and yet it was so. I suddenly found myself extricated from a demonic labyrinth. I again saw the world bright and joyful before me and no longer succumbed to fits of suffocating fear. The spell was broken, I was no longer damned and tormented. I was a schoolboy again, and my whole being sought to regain its peaceful equilibrium as quickly as possible, making a particular effort to repel and forget the ugly, threatening things I had come to know. The whole episode of my guilt and fright slipped from my memory with incredible speed and without apparently leaving any scars or deep impressions behind.

However, today I can understand why I strained to forget my savior so quickly. I fled from the valley of sorrow, my horrible bondage to Kromer, with all the strength at the command of my injured soul: back to where I had been happy and content, back to the lost paradise that was opening up again now, back to the light, untroubled world of mother and father, my sisters, the smell of cleanliness, and the piety of Abel.

Already, the day after my short talk with Demian, when I was fully convinced at last of having regained my freedom and no longer feared losing it again, I did what I had wanted to do so often and desperately before—I confessed. I went to my mother, I showed her the damaged piggy bank filled with play money and I told her for how long I had bound myself through my own guilt to an evil tormentor. She did not understand everything but she saw; she saw my changed expression, heard the change in my tone of voice, and felt that I was cured and had been restored to her.

And now began the feast of my readmittance to the fold, the return of the Prodigal Son. Mother took me to my father, the story was repeated, there were questions and exclamations of surprise, both parents stroked my head and breathed sighs of relief after the long period of oppression. Everything was marvelous, everything happened as the stories I had read said they would, everything resolved itself in wonderful harmony.

I drugged myself on the satisfaction of having regained my peace of mind and the confidence of my parents, I became a most exemplary boy at home, played more than ever with my sisters and during the devotional periods sang all my favorite hymns with the fervor of one who has been saved, who has been converted. It came from my heart, there was nothing false about it.

Still, not everything was back in order. And this is the fact that really accounts for my neglect of Demian. I should have confessed to *him*. The confession would have been less emotional and touching, but it would have been far more fruitful. I had returned to my former, my Edenic world. This was not Demian's world, and he would never have been able to fit into it. He too—though differently from Kromer—was a tempter; he, too, was a link to the second, the evil world with which I no longer wanted to have anything to do. I did not want to sacrifice Abel to glorify Cain, not just now when I had once more become Abel.

Those were the superficial reasons. The inner ones, however, were as follows: I was free of Kromer and the devil's hands but through no power or effort of my own. I had tried to pass through the labyrinth of the world but the way had proved too intricate for me. Now that a friendly hand had extricated me, I retreated, looking neither to the left nor to the right, but went straight to my mother's lap and the security of a pious, sheltered childhood. I turned myself into someone younger, more dependent, more childish than I was. I had to replace my dependence on Kromer with a new one, for I was unable to walk alone. So, in the blindness of my heart, I chose to be dependent on my father and mother, on the old, cherished "world of light," though I knew by now that it was not the only one. If I had not followed this course I would have had to bank on Demian and entrust myself to him. That I did not do so at the time seemed to me to be the result of my justifiable suspicion of his strange ideas; in reality it was entirely because of my fear. For Demian would have been far more exacting than my parents; he would have tried to make me more independent by using persuasion, exhortation, mockery, and sarcasm. I realize today that nothing in the world is more distasteful to a man than to take the path that leads to himself.

Yet six months later I could not resist the temptation and I asked my father during a walk what one was to make of the fact that some people considered Cain a better person than Abel.

He was much taken aback and explained that this was an interpretation entirely lacking in originality, that it had already arisen in Old Testament times and had been taught by a number of sects, one of which were called the "Cainites." But of course this mad doctrine was merely an attempt on the part of the devil to destroy our faith, for, if one believed that Cain was right and Abel in the wrong, then it followed that God had made a mistake; in other words, the God of the Bible was not the right and only one, but a false God. Indeed, the Cainites had taught and preached something of the sort. However, this heresy had long since disappeared from the face of the earth and he was only surprised that a school friend of mine should have heard anything about it. He warned me most seriously against harboring such ideas.

3)   Among Thieves

IF I WANTED TO, I could recall many delicate moments
from my childhood: the sense of being protected that my
parents gave me, my affectionate nature, simply living a
playful, satisfied existence in gentle surroundings. But my
interest centers on the steps that I took to reach myself.
All the moments of calm, the islands of peace whose
magic I felt, I leave behind in the enchanted distance.
Nor do I ask to ever set foot there again.

That is why—as long as I dwell on my childhood—I
will emphasize the things that entered it from outside,
that were new, that impelled me forward or tore me
away.

These impulses always came from the "other world"
and were accompanied by fear, constraint, and a bad conscience. They were always revolutionary and threatened
the calm in which I would gladly have continued to
live.

Then came those years in which I was forced to recognize the existence of a drive within me that had to make

itself small and hide from the world of light. The slowly awakening sense of my own sexuality overcame me, as it does every person, like an enemy and terrorist, as something forbidden, tempting and sinful. What my curiosity sought, what dreams, lust and fear created—the great secret of puberty—did not fit at all into my sheltered childhood. I behaved like everyone else. I led the double life of a child who is no longer a child. My conscious self lived within the familiar and sanctioned world, it denied the new world that dawned within me. Side by side with this I lived in a world of dreams, drives, and desires of a chthonic nature, across which my conscious self desperately built its fragile bridges, for the childhood world within me was falling apart. Like most parents, mine were no help with the new problems of puberty, to which no reference was ever made. All they did was take endless trouble in supporting my hopeless attempts to deny reality and to continue dwelling in a childhood world that was becoming more and more unreal. I have no idea whether parents can be of help, and I do not blame mine. It was my own affair to come to terms with myself and to find my own way, and like most well-brought-up children, I managed it badly.

Everyone goes through this crisis. For the average person this is the point when the demands of his own life come into the sharpest conflict with his environment, when the way forward has to be sought with the bitterest means at his command. Many people experience the dying and rebirth—which is our fate—only this once during their entire life. Their childhood becomes hollow and gradually collapses, everything they love abandons them and they suddenly feel surrounded by the loneliness and mortal cold of the universe. Very many are caught forever in this impasse, and for the rest of their lives cling painfully to an irrevocable past, the dream of the lost paradise —which is the worst and most ruthless of dreams.

But let me return to my story. The sensations and dream images announcing the end of my childhood are too many to be related in full. The important thing was that the "dark world," the "other world," had reappeared. What Franz Kromer had once been was now part of myself.

Several years had gone by since the episode with Kromer. That dramatic time filled with guilt lay far in the past and seemed like a brief nightmare that had quickly vanished. Franz Kromer had long since gone out of my life, I hardly noticed when I happened to meet him in the street. The other important figure in my little tragedy, Max Demian, was never to go out of my life again entirely. Yet for a long time he merely stood at its distant fringes, visible but out of effective range. Only gradually did he come closer, again radiating strength and influence.

I am trying to see what I can remember of Demian at that time. It is quite possible that I didn't talk to him once for a whole year or even longer. I avoided him and he did not impose himself on me in any way. The few instances that we met, he merely nodded to me. Sometimes it even seemed as though his friendliness was faintly tinged with derision or with ironic reproach—but I may have imagined this. The experience that we had shared and the strange influence he had exerted on me at that time were seemingly forgotten by both of us.

I can conjure up what he looked like and now that I begin to recollect, I can see that he was not so far away from me after all and that I did notice him. I can see him on his way to school, alone or with a group of older students, and I see him strange, lonely, and silent, wandering among them like a separate planet, surrounded by an aura all his own, a law unto himself. No one liked him, no one was on intimate terms with him, except his mother, and this relationship, too, seemed not that of a child but of an adult. When they could, the teachers left him to himself; he was a good student but took no particular trouble to please anyone. Now and again we heard of some word, some sarcastic comment or retort he was rumored to have made to a teacher, and which—as gems of provocation and cutting irony—left little to be desired.

As I close my eyes to recollect I can see his image rise up: where was that? Yes, I have it now: in the little alley before our house. One day I saw him standing there, notebook in hand, sketching. He was drawing the old coat of arms with the bird above our entrance. As I stood at the window behind the curtain and watched him, I was deeply astonished by his perceptive, cool, light-skinned face that was turned toward the coat of arms, the face of a man, of a scientist or artist, superior and purposeful, strangely lucid and calm, and with knowing eyes.

And I can see him on another occasion. It was a few weeks later, also in a street. All of us on our way home from school were standing about a fallen horse. It lay in front of a farmer's cart still harnessed to the shaft, snorting pitifully with dilated nostrils and bleeding from a hidden wound so the white dust on one side of the street was stained. As I turned away nauseous I beheld Demian's face. He had not thrust himself forward but was standing farthest back, at ease and as elegantly dressed as usual.

His eyes seemed fixed on the horse's head and again showed that deep, quiet, almost fanatical yet dispassionate absorption. I could not help looking at him for a time and it was then that I felt a very remote and peculiar sensation. I saw Demian's face and I not only noticed that it was not a boy's face but a man's; I also felt or saw that it was not entirely the face of a man either, but had something feminine about it, too. Yet the face struck me at that moment as neither masculine nor childlike, neither old nor young, but somehow a thousand years old, somehow timeless, bearing the scars of an entirely different history than we knew; animals could look like that, or trees, or planets—none of this did I know consciously, I did not feel precisely what I say about it now as an adult, only something of the kind. Perhaps he was handsome, perhaps I liked him, perhaps I also found him repulsive, I could not be sure of that either. All I saw was that he was different from us, he was like an animal or like a spirit or like a picture, he was different, unimaginably different from the rest of us.

My memory fails me and I cannot be sure whether what I have described has not to some extent been drawn from later impressions.

Only several years later did I again come into closer contact with him. Demian had not been confirmed in church with his own age group as was the custom, and this again made him the object of wild rumors. Boys in school repeated the old story about his being Jewish, or more likely a heathen, and others were convinced that both he and his mother were atheists or belonged to some fabulous and disreputable sect. In connection with this I also remember having heard him suspected of being his

mother's lover. Most probably he had been brought up
without any religious instruction whatever, but now this
seemed to be in some way ominous for his future. At any
rate, his mother decided to let him take Confirmation lessons after all, though two years later than his age group.
So it came about that he went to the same Confirmation
class as I did.

For a time I avoided him entirely. I wanted no part of
him; he was surrounded by too many legends and secrets,
but what bothered me most was a feeling of being in-
debted to him that had not left me since the Kromer
affair. I now had enough trouble with secrets of my own,
for the Confirmation lessons coincided with my decisive
enlightenment about sex, and despite all good intentions,
my interest in religious matters was greatly diminished.
What the pastor discussed lay far away in a very holy but
unreal world of its own; these things were no doubt quite
beautiful and precious, but they were by no means as
timely and exciting as the new things I was thinking
about.

The more indifferent this condition made me to the Confirmation lessons, the more I again became preoccupied
with Max Demian. There seemed to be a bond between
us, a bond that I shall have to trace as closely as possible.
As far as I can remember, it began early one morning
while the light still had to be turned on in our classroom.
Our scripture teacher, a pastor, had embarked on the story
of Cain and Abel. I was sleepy and listened with only half
an ear. When the pastor began to hold forth loudly and urgently about Cain's mark I felt almost a physical touch, a
warning, and looking up I saw Max Demian's face half
turned round toward me from one of the front rows, with

a gleaming eye that might express scorn as much as deep thought, you could not be sure. He looked at me for only a moment and suddenly I listened tensely to the pastor's words, heard him speak about Cain and his mark, and deep within me I felt the knowledge that it was not as he was teaching it, that one could look at it differently, that his view was not above criticism.

This one minute re-established the link between me and Demian. And how strange—hardly was I aware of a certain spiritual affinity, when I saw it translated into physical closeness. I had no idea whether he was able to arrange it this way himself or whether it happened only by chance—I still believed firmly in chance at that time—but after a few days Demian suddenly switched seats in Confirmation class and came to sit in front of me (I can still recall it precisely: in the miserable poorhouse air of the over-crowded classroom I loved the scent of fresh soap emanating from his nape) and after a few days he had again changed seats and now sat next to me. There he stayed all winter and spring.

The morning hours had changed completely. They no longer put me to sleep or bored me. I actually looked forward to them. Sometimes both of us listened to the pastor with the utmost concentration and a glance from my neighbor could draw my attention to a remarkable story, an unusual saying. A further glance from him, a special one, could make me critical or doubtful.

Yet all too frequently we paid no attention. Demian was never rude to the teacher or to his fellow students. I never saw him indulge in the usual pranks, not once did I hear him guffaw or gossip during class, and he never incurred a teacher's reprimand. But very quietly, and more with signs and glances than whispering, he contrived to let me share in his activities, and these sometimes were strange.

For instance, he would tell me which of the students interested him and how he studied them. About some of them he had very precise knowledge. He would tell me before class: "When I signal with my thumb So-and-so will turn round and look at us, or will scratch his neck." During the period, when it had almost completely slipped my mind, Max would suddenly make a significant gesture with his thumb. I would glance quickly at the student indicated and each time I saw him perform the desired movement like a puppet on a string. I begged Max to try this out on the pastor but he refused. Only once, when I came to class unprepared and told him that I hoped the pastor would not call on me that day, he helped me. The pastor looked for a student to recite an assigned catechism passage and his eyes sweeping through the room came to rest on my guilty face. Slowly he approached me, his finger pointing at me, my name beginning to form on his lips —when suddenly he became distracted or uneasy, pulled at his shirt collar, stepped up to Demian, who was looking him directly in the eye and seemed to want to ask him something. But he turned away again, cleared his throat a few times, and then called on someone else.

Even though these tricks amused me, I began to notice gradually that my friend frequently played the same game with me. It would happen on my way to school that I would suddenly feel Demian walking not far behind me and when I turned around he was there in fact.

"Can you actually make someone think what you want him to?" I asked him.

He answered readily in his quiet, factual, and adult manner.

"No," he said, "I can't do that. You see, we don't have

free will even though the pastor makes believe we do. A person can neither think what he wants to nor can I make him think what I want to. However, one can study some-one very closely and then one can often know almost exactly what he thinks or feels and then one can also antic-ipate what he will do the next moment. It's simple enough, only people don't know it. Of course you need practice. For example, there is a species of butterfly, a night-moth, in which the females are much less common than the males. The moths breed exactly like all animals, the male fertilizes the female and the female lays the eggs. Now, if you take a female night-moth—many naturalists have tried this experiment—the male moths will visit this fe-male at night, and they will come from hours away. From hours away! Just think! From a distance of several miles all these males sense the only female in the region. One looks for an explanation for this phenomenon but it is not easy. You must assume that they have a sense of smell of some sort like a hunting dog that can pick up and follow a seemingly imperceptible scent. Do you see? Nature abounds with such inexplicable things. But my argument is: if the female moths were as abundant as the males, the latter would not have such a highly developed sense of smell. They've acquired it only because they had to train themselves to have it. If a person were to concentrate all his will power on a certain end, then he would achieve it. That's all. And that also answers your question. Examine a person closely enough and you know more about him than he does himself."

It was on the tip of my tongue to mention "thought reading" and to remind him of the scene with Kromer that lay so far in the past. But this, too, was strange about our relationship: neither he nor I ever alluded to the fact that several years before he had intruded so seriously into my life. It was as though nothing had ever been between us or as though each of us banked on it that the other had forgotten. On one or two occasions it even happened that we caught sight of Kromer somewhere in the street. Yet we neither glanced at each other nor said a word about him.

"What is all this about the will?" I asked. "On the one hand, you say our will isn't free. Then again you say we only need to concentrate our will firmly on some end in order to achieve it. It doesn't make sense. If I'm not master of my own will, then I'm in no position to direct it as I please."

He patted me on the back as he always did when he was pleased with me.

"Good that you ask," he said, laughing. "You should always ask, always have doubts. But the matter is very simple. If, for example, a night-moth were to concentrate its will on flying to a star or on some equally unattainable object, it wouldn't succeed. Only—it wouldn't even try in the first place. A moth confines its search to what has sense and value for it, on what it needs, what is indispensable to its life. And that's how a moth achieves the incredible—it develops a magic sixth sense, which no other creature has. We have a wider scope, greater variety of choice, and wider interests than an animal. But we, too, are confined to a relatively narrow compass which we cannot break out of. If I imagined that I wanted under all circumstances to get to the North Pole, to achieve it I would have to desire it strongly enough so that my whole being was ruled by it. Once that is the case, once you have tried something that you have been ordered to do from within yourself, then you'll be able to accomplish it, then you can harness your will to it like an obedient nag. But if I were to decide to will that the pastor should stop wearing his glasses, it would be useless. That would be making a game of it. But at that time in the fall when I was resolved to move away from my seat in the front row, it wasn't difficult at all. Suddenly there was someone whose name preceded mine in the alphabet and who had been away sick until then and since someone had to make room for him it was me of course because my will was ready to seize the opportunity at once."

"Yes," I said. "I too felt odd at that time. From the moment that we began to take an interest in each other you moved closer and closer to me. But how did that happen? You did not sit next to me right away, first you sat for awhile in the bench in front of me. How did you manage to switch once more?"

"It was like this: I didn't know myself exactly where I wanted to sit but I wanted to shift from my seat in the front row. I only knew that I wanted to sit farther to the back. It was my will to come to sit next to you but I hadn't become conscious of it as yet. At the same time your will accorded with mine and helped me. Only when I found myself sitting in front of you did I realize that my wish was only half fulfilled and that my sole aim was to sit next to you."

"But at that time no one fell ill, no one who had been ill returned, no new student joined the class."

"You're right. But at the time I simply did as I liked and sat down next to you. The boy with whom I changed seats was somewhat surprised but he let me do as I pleased. The pastor, too, once noticed that some sort of change had occurred. Even now something bothers him secretly every time he has to deal with me, for he knows that my name is Demian and that something must be wrong if I, a D, sit way in back in the S's. But that never penetrates his awareness because my will opposes it and because I continuously place obstacles in his path. He keeps noticing that there's something wrong, then he looks at me and tries to puzzle it out. But I have a simple solution to that. Every time his eyes meet mine I stare him down. Very few people can stand that for long. All of them become uneasy. If you want something from someone and you look him firmly in both eyes and he doesn't become ill at ease, give up. You don't have a chance, ever! But that is very rare. I actually know only one person where it doesn't help me."

"Who is that?" I asked quickly.

He looked at me with narrowed eyes, as he did when he became thoughtful. Then he looked away and made no reply. Even though I was terribly curious I could not repeat the question.

I believe he meant his mother. He was said to have a very close relationship with her, yet he never mentioned her name and never took me home with him. I hardly knew what his mother looked like.

Sometimes I attempted to imitate Demian and fix my will with such concentration on something that I was certain to achieve it. There were wishes that seemed urgent enough to me. But nothing happened; it didn't work. I could not bring myself to talk to Demian about it. I wouldn't have been able to confess my wishes to him. And he didn't ask either.

Meantime cracks had begun to appear in my religious

faith. Yet my thinking, which was certainly much influ-
enced by Demian, was very different from that of some of
my fellow students who boasted complete unbelief. On
occasion they would say it was ridiculous, unworthy of a
person to believe in God, that stories like the Trinity and
Virgin Birth were absurd, shameful. It was a scandal that
we were still being fed such nonsense in our time. I did
not share these views. Even though I had my doubts
about certain points, I knew from my childhood the reality of a devout life, as my parents led it, and I knew also
that this was neither unworthy nor hypocritical. On the
contrary, I still stood in the deepest awe of the religious.
Demian, however, had accustomed me to regard and interpret religious stories and dogma more freely, more
individually, even playfully, with more imagination; at
any rate, I always subscribed with pleasure to the interpretations he suggested. Some of it—the Cain business,
for instance—was, of course, too much for me to stomach.
And once during Confirmation class he startled me with
an opinion that was possibly even more daring. The
teacher had been speaking about Golgotha. The biblical
account of the suffering and death of the Savior had made
a deep impression on me since my earliest childhood.
Sometimes, as a little boy, on Good Friday, for instance,
deeply moved by my father's reading of the Passion to us,
I would live in this sorrowful yet beautiful, ghostly, pale,
yet immensely alive world, in Gethsemane and on Golgotha, and when I heard Bach's *St. Matthew Passion* the
dark mighty glow of suffering in this mysterious world
filled me with a mystical sense of trembling. Even today I
find in this music and in his *Actus Tragicus* the essence of
all poetry.

At the end of that class Demian said to me thought-fully: "There's something I don't like about this story, Sinclair. Why don't you read it once more and give it the acid test? There's something about it that doesn't taste right. I mean the business with the two thieves. The three crosses standing next to each other on the hill are most impressive, to be sure. But now comes this sentimental little treatise about the good thief. At first he was a thorough scoundrel, had committed all those awful things and God knows what else, and now he dissolves in tears and celebrates such a tearful feast of self-improvement and remorse! What's the sense of repenting if you're two steps from the grave? I ask you. Once again it's nothing but a priest's fairy tale, saccharine and dishonest, touched up with sentimentality and given a highly edifying background. If you had to pick a friend from between the two thieves or decide which of the two you had rather trust, you most certainly wouldn't select that sniveling convert. No, the other fellow, he's a man of character. He doesn't give a hoot for 'conversion,' which to a man in his position can't be anything but a pretty speech. He follows his destiny to its appointed end and does not turn coward and forswear the devil, who has aided and abetted him until then. He has character, and people with character tend to receive the short end of the stick in biblical stories. Perhaps he's even a descendant of Cain. Don't you agree?"

I was dismayed. Until now I had felt completely at home in the story of the Crucifixion. Now I saw for the first time with how little individuality, with how little power of imagination I had listened to it and read it. Still, Demian's new concept seemed vaguely sinister and threatened to topple beliefs on whose continued existence

I felt I simply had to insist. No, one could not make light of everything, especially not of the most sacred matters.

As usual he noticed my resistance even before I had said anything.

"I know," he said in a resigned tone of voice, "it's the same old story: don't take these stories seriously! But I have to tell you something: this is one of the very places that reveals the poverty of this religion most distinctly. The point is that this God of both Old and New Testaments is certainly an extraordinary figure but not what he purports to represent. He is all that is good, noble, fatherly, beautiful, elevated, sentimental—true! But the world consists of something else besides. And what is left over is ascribed to the devil, this entire slice of world, this entire half is suppressed and hushed up. In exactly the same way they praise God as the father of all life but simply refuse to say a word about our sexual life on which it's all based, describing it whenever possible as sinful, the work of the devil. I have no objection to worshiping this God Jehovah, far from it. But I mean we ought to consider everything sacred, the entire world, not merely this artificially separated half! Thus alongside the divine service we should also have a service for the devil. I feel that would be right. Otherwise you must create for yourself a God that contains the devil too and in front of which you needn't close your eyes when the most natural things in the world take place."

It was most unusual for him to become almost vehement. But at once he smiled and did not probe any further.

His words, however, touched directly on the whole secret of my adolescence, a secret I carried with me every hour of the day and of which I had not said a word to anyone, ever. What Demian had said about God and the devil, about the official godly and the suppressed devilish one, corresponded exactly to my own thoughts, my own myth, my own conception of the world as being divided into two halves—the light and the dark. The realization that my problem was one that concerned all men, a problem of living and thinking, suddenly swept over me and I was overwhelmed by fear and respect as I suddenly saw and felt how deeply my own personal life and opinions were immersed in the eternal stream of great ideas. Though it offered some confirmation and gratification, the realization was not really a joyful one. It was hard and had a harsh taste because it implied responsibility and no longer being allowed to be a child; it meant standing on one's own feet.

Revealing a deep secret for the first time in my life, I told my friend of my conception of the "two worlds." He saw immediately that my deepest feelings accorded with his own. But it was not his way to take advantage of something like that. He listened to me more attentively than he had ever before and peered into my eyes so that I was forced to avert mine. For I noticed in his gaze again that strange animal-like look, expressing timelessness and unimaginable age.

"We'll talk more about it some other time," he said forbearingly. "I can see that your thoughts are deeper than you yourself are able to express. But since this is so, you know, don't you, that you've never lived what you are thinking and that isn't good. Only the ideas that we actually live are of any value. You knew all along that your sanctioned world was only half the world and you tried to suppress the second half the same way the priests and teachers do. You won't succeed. No one succeeds in this once he has begun to think."

This went straight to my heart.

"But there are forbidden and ugly things in the world!" I almost shouted. "You can't deny that. And they are forbidden, and we must renounce them. Of course I know that murder and all kinds of vices exist in the world but should I become a criminal just because they exist?"

"We won't be able to find all the answers today," Max soothed me. "Certainly you shouldn't go kill somebody or rape a girl, no! But you haven't reached the point where you can understand the actual meaning of 'permitted' and 'forbidden.' You've only sensed part of the truth. You will feel the other part, too, you can depend on it. For instance, for about a year you have had to struggle with a drive that is stronger than any other and which is considered 'forbidden.' The Greeks and many other peoples, on the other hand, elevated this drive, made it divine and celebrated it in great feasts. What is forbidden, in other words, is not something eternal; it can change. Anyone can sleep with a woman as soon as he's been to a pastor with her and has married her, yet other races do it differently, even nowadays. That is why each of us has to find out for himself what is permitted and what is forbidden—forbidden for him. It's possible for one never to transgress a single law and still be a bastard. And vice versa. Actually it's only a question of convenience. Those who are too lazy and comfortable to think for themselves and be their own judges obey the laws. Others sense their own laws within them; things are forbidden to them that every honorable man will do any day in the year and other things are allowed to them that are generally despised. Each person must stand on his own feet."

Suddenly he seemed to regret having said so much and fell silent. I could already sense what he felt at such moments. Though he delivered his ideas in a pleasant and perfunctory manner, he still could not stand conversation for its own sake, as he once told me. In my case, however, he sensed—besides genuine interest—too much playfulness, too much sheer pleasure in clever gabbing, or something of the sort; in short, a lack of complete commitment.

As I reread the last two words I have just written—complete commitment—a scene leaps to mind, the most impressive I ever experienced with Max Demian in those days when I was still half a child.

Confirmation day was approaching and our lessons had the Last Supper for their topic. This was a matter of importance to the pastor and he took great pains explaining it to us. One could almost taste the solemn mood during those last hours of instruction. And of all times it had to be now that my thoughts were farthest from class, for they were fixed on my friend. While I looked ahead to being confirmed, which was explained to us as a solemn acceptance into the community of the church, I could not help thinking that the value of this religious instruction consisted for me not in what I had learned, but in the proximity and influence of Max Demian. It was not into the church that I was ready to be received but into something entirely different—into an order of thought and personality that must exist somewhere on earth and whose representative or messenger I took to be my friend.

I tried to suppress this idea—I was anxious to involve

myself in the Confirmation ceremony with a certain dignity, and this dignity seemed not to agree very well with my new idea. Yet, no matter what I did, the thought was present and gradually it became firmly linked with the approaching ceremony. I was ready to enact it differently from the others, for it was to signify my acceptance into a world of thought as I had come to know it through Demian.

On one of those days it happened that we were having an argument just before class. My friend was tight-lipped and seemed to take no pleasure in my talk, which probably was self-important as well as precocious.

"We talk too much," he said with unwonted seriousness. "Clever talk is absolutely worthless. All you do in the process is lose yourself. And to lose yourself is a sin. One has to be able to crawl completely inside oneself, like a tortoise."

Then we entered the classroom. The lesson began and I made an effort to pay attention. Demian did not distract me. After a while I began to sense something odd from the side where he sat, an emptiness or coolness or something similar, as though the seat next to me had suddenly become vacant. When the feeling became oppressive I turned to look.

There I saw my friend sitting upright, his shoulders braced back as usual. Nonetheless, he looked completely different and something emanated from him, something surrounded him that was unknown to me. I first thought he had his eyes closed but then saw they were open. Yet they were not focused on anything, it was an unseeing gaze—they seemed transfixed with looking inward or into a great distance. He sat there completely motionless, not even seeming to breathe; his mouth might have been carved from wood or stone. His face was pale, uniformly pale like a stone, and his brown hair was the part of him that seemed closest to being alive. His hands lay before him on the bench, lifeless and still as objects, like stones or fruit, pale, motionless yet not limp, but like good, strong pods sheathing a hidden, vigorous life.

I trembled at the sight. Dead, I thought, almost saying it aloud. My spellbound eyes were fixed on his face, on this pale stone mask, and I felt: this is the real Demian. When he walked beside me or talked to me—that was only half of him, someone who periodically plays a role, adapts himself, who out of sheer complaisance does as the others do. The real Demian, however, looked like this, as primeval, animal, marble, beautiful and cold, dead yet secretly filled with fabulous life. And around him this quiet emptiness, this ether, interstellar space, this lonely death!

Now he has gone completely into himself, I felt, and I trembled. Never had I been so alone. I had no part in him; he was inaccessible; he was more remote from me than if he had been on the most distant island in the world.

I could hardly grasp it that no one besides me noticed him! Everyone should have looked at him, everyone should have trembled! But no one heeded him. He sat there like a statue, and, I thought, proud as an idol! A fly lighted on his forehead and scurried across his nose and lips—not a muscle twitched.

Where was he now? What was he thinking? What did he feel? Was he in heaven or was he in hell?

I was unable to put a question to him. At the end of the period, when I saw him alive and breathing again, as his glance met mine, he was the same as he had been before. Where did he come from? Where had he been? He seemed tired. His face was no longer pale, his hands moved again, but now the brown hair was without luster, as though lifeless.

During the next few days, I began a new exercise in my bedroom. I would sit rigid in a chair, make my eyes rigid too, and stay completely motionless and see how long I could keep it up, and what I would feel. I only felt very tired and my eyelids itched.

Shortly afterwards we were confirmed, an event that calls forth no important memories whatever.

Now everything changed. My childhood world was breaking apart around me. My parents eyed me with a certain embarrassment. My sisters had become strangers to me. A disenchantment falsified and blunted my usual feelings and joys: the garden lacked fragrance, the woods held no attraction for me, the world stood around me like a clearance sale of last year's secondhand goods, insipid, all its charm gone. Books were so much paper, music a grating noise. That is the way leaves fall around a tree in autumn, a tree unaware of the rain running down its sides, of the sun or the frost, and of life gradually retreating inward. The tree does not die. It waits.

It had been decided that I would be sent away to a boarding school at the end of the vacation; for the first time I would be away from home. Sometimes my mother approached me with particular tenderness, as if already taking leave of me ahead of time, intent on inspiring love, homesickness, the unforgettable in my heart. Demian was away on a trip. I was alone.

4) Beatrice

At the end of the holidays, and without having seen my friend again, I went to St. ———. My parents accompanied me and entrusted me to the care of a boy's boarding-house run by one of the teachers at the preparatory school. They would have been struck dumb with horror had they known into what world they were letting me wander.

The question remained: was I eventually to become a good son and useful citizen or did my nature point in an altogether different direction? My last attempt to achieve happiness in the shadow of the paternal home had lasted a long time, had on occasion almost succeeded, but had completely failed in the end.

The peculiar emptiness and isolation that I came to feel for the first time after Confirmation (oh, how familiar it was to become afterwards, this desolate, thin air!) passed only very slowly. My leave-taking from home was surprisingly easy, I was almost ashamed that I did not feel more nostalgic. My sisters wept for no reason; my eyes remained dry. I was astonished at myself. I had always been an emotional and essentially good child. Now I had completely changed. I behaved with utter indifference to the world outside and for days on end voices within preoccupied me, inner streams, the forbidden dark streams that roared below the surface. I had grown several inches in the last half year and I walked lanky and half-finished through the world. I had lost any charm I might ever have had and felt that no one could possibly love me the way I was. I certainly had no love for myself. Often I felt a great longing for Max Demian, but no less often I hated him, accusing him of having caused the impoverishment of my life that held me in its sway like a foul disease.

I was neither liked nor respected in my boys' boardinghouse. I was teased to begin with, then avoided and looked upon as a sneak and an unwelcome oddity. I fell in with this role, even exaggerated it, and grumbled myself into a self-isolation that must have appeared to outsiders like permanent and masculine contempt of the world, whereas, in truth, I often secretly succumbed to consuming fits of melancholy and despair. In school I managed to get by on the knowledge accumulated in my previous class—the present one lagged somewhat behind the one I had left—and I began to regard the students in my age group contemptuously as mere children.

It went on like this for a year or more. The first few visits back home left me cold. I was glad when I could leave again.

It was the beginning of November. I had become used to taking short meditative walks during all kinds of weather, walks on which I often enjoyed a kind of rapture tinged with melancholy, scorn of the world and self-hatred. Thus I roamed in the foggy dusk one evening through the town. The broad avenue of a public park stood deserted, beckoning me to enter; the path lay thickly carpeted with fallen leaves which I stirred angrily with my feet. There was a damp, bitter smell, and distant trees, shadowy as ghosts, loomed huge out of the mist.

I stopped irresolute at the far end of the avenue: staring into the dark foliage I greedily breathed the humid fragrance of decay and dying to which something within me responded with greeting.

Someone stepped out of one of the side paths, his coat billowing as he walked. I was about to continue when a voice called out:

"Hello, Sinclair."

He came up to me. It was Alfons Beck, the oldest boy in our boardinghouse. I was always glad to see him, had nothing against him except that he treated me, and all others who were younger, with an element of ironic and avuncular condescension. He was reputed to be strong as a bear and to have the teacher in our house completely under his thumb. He was the hero of many a student rumor.

"Well, what are you doing here?" he called out affably in that tone the bigger boys affected when they occasionally condescended to talk to one of us. "I'll bet anything you're making a poem."

"Wouldn't think of it," I replied brusquely.

He laughed out loud, walked beside me, and made small talk in a way I hadn't been used to for a long time.

"You don't need to be afraid that I wouldn't understand, Sinclair. There's something to walking with autumnal thoughts through the evening fog. One likes to compose poems at a time like that, I know. About moribund nature, of course, and one's lost youth, which resembles it. Heinrich Heine, for example."

"I'm not as sentimental as all that," I defended myself.

"All right, let's drop the subject. But it seems to me that in weather like this a man does the right thing when he looks for a quiet place where he can drink a good glass of wine or something. Will you join me? I happen to be all by myself at the moment. Or would you rather not? I don't want to be the one who leads you astray, mon vieux, that is, in case you happen to be the kind that keeps to the straight and narrow."

Soon afterwards we were sitting in a small dive at the edge of town, drinking a wine of doubtful quality and clinking the thick glasses. I didn't much like it to begin with, but at least it was something new. Soon, however, unused to the wine, I became very loquacious. It was as though an interior window had opened through which the world sparkled. For how long, for how terribly long hadn't I really talked to anyone? My imagination began to run away with me and eventually I even popped out with the story of Cain and Abel.

Beck listened with evident pleasure—finally here was someone to whom I was able to give something! He patted me on the shoulder, called me one hell of a fellow, and my heart swelled ecstatically at this opportunity to luxuriate in the release of a long pent-up need for talk and communication, for acknowledgment from an older boy. When he called me a damned clever little bastard, the words ran like sweet wine into my soul. The world glowed in new colors, thoughts gushed out of a hundred audacious springs. The fire of enthusiasm flared up within me. We discussed our teachers and fellow students and it

seemed to me that we understood each other perfectly.
We talked about the Greeks and the pagans in general
and Beck very much wanted me to confess to having slept
with girls. This was out of my league. I hadn't experienced anything, certainly nothing worth telling. And what
I had felt, what I had constructed in imagination, ached
within me but had not been loosened or made communi-
cable by the wine. Beck knew much more about girls, so I
listened to his exploits without being able to say a word. I
heard incredible things. Things I had never thought possible became everyday reality, seemed normal. Alfons
Beck, who was eighteen, seemed to be able to draw on a
vast body of experience. For instance, he had learned that
it was a funny thing about girls, they just wanted to flirt,
which was all very well, but not the real thing. For the
real thing one could hope for greater success with women.
Women were much more reasonable. Mrs. Jaggelt, for
example, who owned the stationery store, well, with her
one could talk business, and all the things that had happened behind her counter wouldn't fit into a book.

I sat there enchanted and also dumbfounded. Certainly,
I could never have loved Mrs. Jaggelt—yet the news was
incredible. There seemed to be hidden sources of pleasure, at least for the older boys, of which I had not even
dreamed. Something about it didn't sound right, and it
tasted less appealing and more ordinary than love, I felt,
was supposed to taste—but at least: this was reality, this
was life and adventure, and next to me sat someone who
had experienced it, to whom it seemed normal.

Once it had reached this height, our conversation began
to taper off. I was no longer the damned clever little
bastard; I'd shrunk to a mere boy listening to a man. Yet

all the same—compared with what my life had been for months—this was delicious, this was paradise. Besides, it was, as I began to realize only gradually, very much prohibited—from our presence in the bar to the subject of our talk. At least for me it smacked of rebellion.

I can remember that night with remarkable clarity. We started on our way home through the damp, past gas lamps dimly lighting the late night: for the first time in my life I was drunk. It was not pleasant. In fact it was most painful, yet it had something, a thrill, a sweetness of rebellious orgy, that was life and spirit. Beck did a good job taking charge of me, even though he cursed me bitterly as a "bloody beginner," and half led, half carried me home. There he succeeded in smuggling me through an open window in the hallway.

The sober reality to which I awoke after a brief death-like sleep coincided with a painful and senseless depression. I sat up in bed, still wearing my shirt. The rest of my clothes, strewn about on the floor, reeked of tobacco and vomit. Between fits of headache, nausea, and a raging thirst an image came to mind which I had not viewed for a long time: I visualized my parents' house, my home, my father and mother, my sisters, the garden. I could see the familiar bedroom, the school, the market place, could see Demian and the Confirmation classes—everything was wonderful, godly pure, and everything, all of this—as I realized now—had still been mine yesterday, a few hours ago, had waited for me; yet now, at this very hour, everything looked ravaged and damned, was mine no longer, rejected me, regarded me with disgust. Everything dear and intimate, everything my parents had given me as far back as the distant gardens of my childhood, every kiss

from my mother, every Christmas, each devout, light-
filled Sunday morning at home, each and every flower in
the garden—everything had been laid waste, everything
had been trampled on *by me!* If the arm of the law had
reached out for me now, had bound and gagged me and
led me to the gallows as the scum of the earth and a
desecrator of the temple, I would not have objected,
would have gladly gone, would have considered it just
and fair.

So that's what I looked like inside! I who was going
about contemptuous of the world! I who was proud in
spirit and shared Demian's thoughts! That's what I looked
like, a piece of excrement, a filthy swine, drunk and filthy,
loathsome and callow, a vile beast brought low by hideous appetites. That's what I looked like, I, who came out
of such pure gardens where everything was cleanliness,
radiance, and tenderness, I, who had loved the music of
Bach and beautiful poetry. With nausea and outrage I
could still hear my life, drunk and unruly, sputtering out
of me in idiotic laughter, in jerks and fits. There I was.

In spite of everything, I almost reveled in my agonies. I
had been blind and insensible and my heart had been
silent for so long, had cowered impoverished in a corner,
that even this self-accusation, this dread, all these horrible
feelings were welcome. At least it was feeling of some
kind, at least there were some flames, the heart at least
flickered. Confusedly I felt something like liberation amid
my misery.

Meanwhile, viewed from the outside, I was going rapidly downhill. My first drunken frenzy was soon followed by others. There was much going to bars and
carousing in our school. I was one of the youngest to take

part, yet soon enough I was not merely a fledgling whom one grudgingly took along, I had become the ringleader and star, a notorious and daring bar crawler. Once again I belonged entirely to the world of darkness and to the devil, and in this world I had the reputation of being one hell of a fellow.

Nonetheless, I felt wretched. I lived in an orgy of self-destruction and, while my friends regarded me as a leader and as a damned sharp and funny fellow, deep down inside me my soul grieved. I can still remember tears springing to my eyes when I saw children playing in the street on Sunday morning as I emerged from a bar, children with freshly combed hair and dressed in their Sunday best. Those friends who sat with me in the lowest dives among beer puddles and dirty tables I amused with remarks of unprecedented cynicism, often even shocked them; yet in my inmost heart I was in awe of everything I belittled and lay weeping before my soul, my past, my mother, before God.

There was good reason why I never became one with my companions, why I felt alone among them and was therefore able to suffer so much. I was a barroom hero and cynic to satisfy the taste of the most brutal. I displayed wit and courage in my ideas and remarks about teachers, school, parents, and church. I could also bear to hear the filthiest stories and even ventured an occasional one myself, but I never accompanied my friends when they visited women. I was alone and was filled with intense longing for love, a hopeless longing, while, to judge by my talk, I should have been a hard-boiled sensualist. No one was more easily hurt, no one more bashful than I.

And when I happened to see the young well-brought-up girls of the town walking in front of me, pretty and clean, innocent and graceful, they seemed like wonderful pure dreams, a thousand times too good for me. For a time I could not even bring myself to enter Mrs. Jaggelt's stationery store because I blushed looking at her remembering what Alfons Beck had told me.

The more I realized that I was to remain perpetually lonely and different within my new group of friends the less I was able to break away. I really don't know any longer whether boozing and swaggering actually ever gave me any pleasure. Moreover, I never became so used to drinking that I did not always feel embarrassing after-effects. It was all as if I were somehow under a compulsion to do these things. I simply did what I had to do, because I had no idea what to do with myself otherwise. I was afraid of being alone for long, was afraid of the many tender and chaste moods that would overcome me, was afraid of the thoughts of love surging up in me.

What I missed above all else was a friend. There were two or three fellow students whom I could have cared for, but they were in good standing and my vices had long been an open secret. They avoided me. I was regarded by and large as a hopeless rebel whose ground was slipping from under his feet. The teachers were well-informed about me, I had been severely punished several times, my final expulsion seemed merely a matter of time. I realized myself that I had become a poor student, but I wriggled strenuously through one exam after the other, always feeling that it couldn't go on like this much longer.

There are numerous ways in which God can make us

lonely and lead us back to ourselves. This was the way He dealt with me at that time. It was like a bad dream. I can see myself: crawling along in my odious and unclean way, across filth and slime, across broken beer glasses and through cynically wasted nights, a spellbound dreamer, restless and racked. There are dreams in which on your way to the princess you become stuck in quagmires, in back alleys full of foul odors and refuse. That was how it was with me. In this unpleasant fashion I was condemned to become lonely, and I raised between myself and my childhood a locked gateway to Eden with its pitilessly resplendent host of guardians. It was a beginning, an awakening of nostalgia for my former self.

Yet I had not become so callous as not to be startled into twinges of fear when my father, alarmed by my tutor's letters, appeared for the first time in St. ——— and confronted me unexpectedly. Later on that winter, when he came a second time, nothing could move me any more, I let him scold and entreat me, let him remind me of my mother. Finally toward the end of the meeting he became quite angry and said if I didn't change he would have me expelled from the school in disgrace and placed in a reformatory. Well, let him! When he went away that time I felt sorry for him; he had accomplished nothing, he had not found a way to me—and at moments I felt that it served him right.

I could not have cared less what became of me. In my odd and unattractive fashion, going to bars and bragging was my way of quarreling with the world—this was my way of protesting. I was ruining myself in the process but at times I understood the situation as follows: if the world

had no use for people like me, if it did not have a better
place and higher tasks for them, well, in that case,
people like me would go to pot, and the loss would be the
world's.

Christmas vacation was a joyless affair that year. My
mother was deeply startled when she saw me. I had shot
up even more and my lean face looked gray and wasted,
with slack features and inflamed eyes. The first touch of a
mustache and the eyeglasses I had just begun wearing
made me look odder still. My sisters shied away and gig-
gled. Everything was most unedifying. Disagreeable and
bitter was the talk I had with my father in his study,
disagreeable exchanging greetings with a handful of relatives, and particularly unpleasant was Christmas Eve itself. Ever since I had been a little child this had been
the great day in our house. The evening was a festivity of
love and gratitude, when the bond between child and
parents was renewed. This time everything was merely
oppressive and embarrassing. As usual my father read
aloud the passage about the shepherds in the fields
"watching their flocks," as usual my sisters stood radiantly
before a table decked with gifts, but father's voice
sounded disgruntled, his face looked old and strained, and
mother was sad. Everything seemed out of place: the
presents and Christmas greetings, Gospel reading and the
lit-up tree. The gingerbread smelled sweet; it exuded a
host of memories which were even sweeter. The fragrance
of the Christmas tree told of a world that no longer existed. I longed for evening and for the holidays to be
over.

It went on like this the entire winter. Only a short while

back I had been given a stern warning by the teachers'
council and been threatened with expulsion. It couldn't go
on much longer. Well, I didn't care.

I held a very special grudge against Max Demian,
whom I hadn't seen again even once. I had written him
twice during my first few months in St. ——— but had
received no reply; so I had not called on him during the
holidays.

In the same park in which I had met Alfons Beck in the
fall, a girl came to my attention in early spring as the
thorn hedges began to bud. I had taken a walk by myself,
my head filled with vile thoughts and worries—for my
health had deteriorated—and to make matters worse I
was perpetually in financial difficulties, owed friends con-
siderable sums and had thus continually to invent expend-
itures so as to receive money from home. In a number of
stores I had allowed bills to mount for cigars and similar
things. Not that this worried me much. If my existence
was about to come to a sudden end anyway—if I drowned
myself or was sent to the reformatory—a few small ex-
tras didn't make much difference. Yet I was forced to live
face to face with these unpleasant details: they made me
wretched.

On that spring day in the park I saw a young woman
who attracted me. She was tall and slender, elegantly
dressed, and had an intelligent and boyish face. I liked
her at once. She was my type and began to fill my imagination. She probably was not much older than I but
seemed far more mature, well-defined, a full-grown
woman, but with a touch of exuberance and boyishness in
her face, and this was what I liked above all.

I had never managed to approach a girl with whom I had fallen in love, nor did I manage in this case. But the impression she made on me was deeper than any previous one had been and the infatuation had a profound influence on my life.

Suddenly a new image had risen up before me, a lofty and cherished image. And no need, no urge was as deep or as fervent within me as the craving to worship and admire. I gave her the name Beatrice, for, even though I had not read Dante, I knew about Beatrice from an English painting of which I owned a reproduction. It showed a young pre-Raphaelite woman, long-limbed and slender, with long head and etherealized hands and features. My beautiful young woman did not quite resemble her, even though she, too, revealed that slender and boyish figure which I loved, and something of the ethereal, soulful quality of her face.

Although I never addressed a single word to Beatrice, she exerted a profound influence on me at that time. She raised her image before me, she gave me access to a holy shrine, she transformed me into a worshiper in a temple. From one day to the next I stayed clear of all bars and nocturnal exploits. I could be alone with myself again and enjoyed reading and going for long walks.

My sudden conversion drew a good deal of mockery in its wake. But now I had something I loved and venerated, I had an ideal again, life was rich with intimations of mystery and a feeling of dawn that made me immune to all taunts. I had come home again to myself, even if only as the slave and servant of a cherished image.

I find it difficult to think back to that time without a certain fondness. Once more I was trying most strenuously to construct an intimate "world of light" for myself out of the shambles of a period of devastation; once more I sacrificed everything within me to the aim of banishing darkness and evil from myself. And, furthermore, this present "world of light" was to some extent my own creation; it was no longer an escape, no crawling back to mother and the safety of irresponsibility; it was a new duty, one I had invented and desired on my own, with responsibility and self-control. My sexuality, a torment from which I was in constant flight, was to be transfigured into spirituality and devotion by this holy fire. Everything dark and hateful was to be banished, there were to be no more tortured nights, no excitement before lascivious pictures, no eavesdropping at forbidden doors, no lust. In place of all this I raised my altar to the image of Beatrice, and by consecrating myself to her I consecrated myself to the spirit and to the gods, sacrificing that part of life which I withdrew from the forces of darkness to those of light. My goal was not joy but purity, not happiness but beauty, and spirituality.

This cult of Beatrice completely changed my life. Yesterday a precocious cynic, today I was an acolyte whose aim was to become a saint. I not only avoided the bad life to which I had become accustomed, I sought to transform myself by introducing purity and nobility into every aspect of my life. In this connection I thought of my eating and drinking habits, my language and dress. I began my mornings with cold baths which cost me a great effort at first. My behavior became serious and dignified; I carried myself stiffly and assumed a slow and dignified gait. It may have looked comic to outsiders but to me it was a genuine act of worship.

Of all the new practices in which I sought to express my new conviction, one became truly important to me. I began to paint. The starting point for this was that the reproduction of the English picture I owned did not resemble my Beatrice closely enough. I wanted to try to paint her portrait for myself. With new joy and hopefulness I bought beautiful paper, paints, and brushes and carried them to my room—I had just been given one of my own—and prepared my palette, glass, porcelain dishes and pencils. The delicate tempera colors in the little tubes I had bought delighted me. Among them was a fiery chrome green that, I think, I can still see today as it flashed up for the first time in the small white dish.

I began with great care. Painting the likeness of a face was difficult. I wanted to try myself out first on something else. I painted ornaments, flowers, small imagined landscapes: a tree by a chapel, a Roman bridge with cypress trees. Sometimes I became so completely immersed in this game that I was as happy as a little child with his paintbox. Finally I set out on my portrait of Beatrice.

A few attempts failed completely and I discarded them. The more I sought to imagine the face of the girl I had encountered here and there on the street the less successful I was. Finally I gave up the attempt and contented myself with giving in to my imagination and intuition that arose spontaneously from the first strokes, as though out of the paint and brush themselves. It was a dream face that emerged and I was not dissatisfied with it. Yet I persisted and every new sketch was more distinct, approximated more nearly the type I desired, even if it in no way reproduced reality.

I grew more and more accustomed to idly drawing lines

with a dreaming paintbrush and to coloring areas for which I had no model in mind, that were the result of playful fumblings of my subconscious. Finally, one day I produced, almost without knowing it, a face to which I responded more strongly than I had to any of the others. It was not the face of that girl—it wasn't supposed to be that any longer. It was something else, something unreal, yet it was no less valuable to me. It looked more like a boy's face than a girl's, the hair was not flaxen like that of my pretty girl, but dark brown with a reddish hue. The chin was strong and determined, the mouth like a red flower. As a whole it was somewhat stiff and masklike but it was impressive and full of a secret life of its own.

As I sat down in front of the completed painting, it had an odd effect on me. It resembled a kind of image of God or a holy mask, half male, half female, ageless, as purposeful as it was dreamy, as rigid as it was secretly alive. This face seemed to have a message for me, it belonged to me, it was asking something of me. It bore a resemblance to someone, yet I did not know whom.

For a time this portrait haunted my thoughts and shared my life. I kept it locked in a drawer so that no one would take it and taunt me with it. But as soon as I was alone in my small room I took it out and communed with it. In the evening I pinned it on the wall facing my bed and gazed on it until I fell asleep and in the morning it was the first thing my eyes opened on.

It was precisely at this time that I again began having many dreams, as I had always had as a child. It felt as though I had not dreamed for years. Now the dreams returned with entirely new images, and time after time the portrait appeared among them, alive and eloquent, friendly or hostile to me, sometimes distorted into a grimace, sometimes infinitely beautiful, harmonious, and noble.

Then one morning, as I awoke from one of these dreams, I suddenly recognized it. It looked at me as though it were fabulously familiar and seemed to call out my name. It seemed to know who I was, like a mother, as if its eyes had been fixed on me since the beginning of time. With a quivering heart I stared at the sheet, the close brown hair, the half-feminine mouth, the pronounced forehead with the strange brightness (it had dried this way of its own accord) and I felt myself coming nearer and nearer to the recognition, the rediscovery, the knowledge.

I leapt out of bed, stepped up to the face, and from inches away looked into its wide-open, greenish, rigid eyes, the right one slightly higher than the left. All at once the right eye twitched, ever so faintly and delicately but unmistakably, and I was able to recognize the picture. . . .

Why had it taken me so long? It was Demian's face.

Later I often compared the portrait with Demian's true features as I remembered them. They were by no means the same even though there was a resemblance. Nonetheless, it was Demian.

Once the early-summer sun slanted oblique and red into a window that faced westward. Dusk was growing in my room. It occurred to me to pin the portrait of Beatrice, or Demian, at the window crossbar and to observe the evening sun shine through it. The outlines of the face became blurred but the red-rimmed eyes, the brightness on the forehead, and the bright red mouth glowed deep and wild from the surface. I sat facing it for a long time, even after the sun had faded, and gradually I began to sense that this was neither Beatrice nor Demian but myself. Not that the picture resembled me—I did not feel that it should—but it was what determined my life, it was my inner self, my fate or my *daemon*. That's what my friend would look like if I were to find one ever again. That's what the woman I would love would look like if ever I were to love one. That's what my life and death would be like, this was the tone and rhythm of my fate.

During those weeks I had begun to read a book that made a more lasting impression on me than anything I had read before. Even later in life I have rarely experienced a book more intensely, except perhaps Nietzsche. It was a volume of Novalis, containing letters and aphorisms of which I understood only a few but which nevertheless held an inexpressible attraction for me. One of the aphorisms occurred to me now and I wrote it under the picture: "Fate and temperament are two words for one and the same concept." That was clear to me now.

I often caught sight of the girl I called Beatrice but I felt no emotion during these encounters, only a gentle harmony, a presentiment: you and I are linked, but not you, only your picture; you are a part of my fate.

My longing for Max Demian overwhelmed me again. I had had no news of him for years. Once I had met him during a vacation. I realized now that I suppressed this brief encounter in my notes and I realize that it was done out of vanity and shame. I have to make up for it.

Thus, during one of my holidays as I strolled through my home town, wearing the blasé, always slightly weary expression of my bar-crawling days, peering into the same old, despised faces of the philistines, I saw my former friend walking toward me. I had hardly seen him when I flinched. At the same moment I could not help thinking of Franz Kromer. If only Demian had really forgotten that episode! It was so unpleasant to be obligated to him. It was actually a silly children's story but an obligation nonetheless. . . .

He appeared to wait: would I greet him? When I did so as casually as possible he stretched out his hand. Yes, that was his grip! As firm, warm yet cool, and virile as ever!

He scrutinized my face and said: "You've grown, Sinclair." He himself seemed quite the same, as old or as young as ever.

He joined me and we took a walk, but talked of only inconsequential matters. It occurred to me that I had written him several times without getting a reply. I hoped that he'd forgotten that too, those stupid letters! He did not mention them.

At that time I had not yet met Beatrice and there was no portrait. I was still in the midst of my drunken period. At the outskirts of town I asked him to join me for a glass of wine and he did so. At once I made a big show of ordering a whole bottle, filled his glass, clinked mine with his, and displayed my great familiarity with student drinking customs by downing the first glass in one swallow.

"You spend a lot of time in bars, do you?" he asked.

"Well, yes," I replied. "What else is there to do? In the end it's more fun than anything else."

"You think? Maybe so. One part of it is of course very fine—the intoxication, the bacchanalian element. But I think most people that frequent bars have lost that entirely. It seems to me that going to bars is something genuinely philistine. Yes, for one night, with burning torches, a real wild drunk! But again and again, one little glass after the other, I wonder whether that's the real thing or not? Can you see Faust sitting night after night stooped over the bar?"

I took a swallow and looked at him with hostility.

"Well, not everybody's Faust," I said curtly.

He looked at me somewhat taken aback.

Then he laughed at me in his old lively and superior fashion. "Well, let's not fight over it! In any case, the life of a drunk is presumably livelier than that of the ordinary well-behaved citizen. And then—I read that once somewhere—the life of a hedonist is the best preparation for becoming a mystic. People like St. Augustine are always the ones that become visionaries. He, too, was first a sensualist and man of the world."

I distrusted him and didn't want him to gain the upper hand under any circumstance. So I said superciliously: "Well, everybody to his own taste. As for me, I've no ambition to become a visionary or anything of the sort."

Demian gave me a brief shrewd look out of half-closed eyes.

"My dear Sinclair," he said slowly, "I didn't intend to tell you anything disagreeable. Besides—neither of us knows why you happen to be drinking wine at this moment. That which is within you and directs your life knows already. It's good to realize that within us there is someone who knows everything, wills everything, does everything better than we ourselves. But excuse me, I must go home."

We exchanged brief good-bys. I stayed on moodily and finished the bottle. When I wanted to leave I discovered that Demian had paid the bill—which put me in an even worse humor.

My thoughts returned to this small incident with Demian. I could not forget him. And the words he said to me in that bar at the edge of town would come to mind, strangely fresh and intact: "It's good to realize that within us there is someone who knows everything."

How I longed for Demian. I had no idea where he was nor how I could reach him. All I knew was that he was presumably studying at some university and that his mother had left town after he completed preparatory school.

I tried to remember whatever I could of Max Demian, reaching back as far as the Kromer episode. How much of what he had said to me over the years returned to mind, was still meaningful today, was appropriate and concerned me! And what he had said on our last and quite disagreeable meeting about a wasted life leading to sainthood suddenly also stood clearly before me. Wasn't that exactly what had happened to me? Hadn't I lived in drunkenness and squalor, dazed and lost, until just the opposite had come alive in me with a new zest for life, the longing for purity, the yearning for the sacred?

So I continued to pursue these memories. Night had long since come and now rain was falling. In my memories, too, I heard the rain: it was the hour under the chestnut trees when he had probed me about Franz Kromer and guessed my first secrets. One incident after another came back to me, conversations on the way to school, the Confirmation classes, and last of all my first meeting with him. What had we talked about? I couldn't find it at once, but I gave myself time, concentrating intensely. And now even that returned. We had stood before my parents' house after he had told me his version of the story of Cain. Then he had mentioned the old, half-hidden coat of arms situated in the keystone above our entrance. He had said that such things interested him and that one ought to attend to them.

That night I dreamed of Demian and the coat of arms. It kept changing continuously. Demian held it in his hand, often it was diminutive and gray, often powerful and varicolored, but he explained to me that it was always one and the same thing. In the end he obliged me to eat the coat of arms! When I had swallowed it, I felt to my horror that the heraldic bird was coming to life inside me, had begun to swell up and devour me from within. Deathly afraid I started up in bed, awoke.

I was wide awake; it was the middle of the night and I could hear rain pouring into the room. As I got up to close the window I stepped on something that shone bright on the floor. In the morning I discovered that it had been my painting. It lay in a puddle and the paper had warped. I placed it between two sheets of blotting paper inside a heavy book. When I looked at it again the next day it was dry, but had changed. The red mouth had faded and contracted a little. It now looked exactly like Demian's mouth.

I set about painting a fresh picture of the heraldic bird. I could not remember distinctly what it looked like and certain details, as I knew, could not be made out even from close up, because the thing was old and had often been painted over. The bird stood or perched on something, perhaps on a flower or on a basket or a nest, or on a treetop. I couldn't trouble myself over this detail and began with what I could visualize clearly. Out of an indistinct need I at once began to employ loud colors, painting the bird's head a golden yellow. Whenever the mood took me, I worked on the picture, bringing it to completion in several days.

Now it represented a bird of prey with a proud aquiline sparrow hawk's head, half its body stuck in some dark globe out of which it was struggling to free itself as though from a giant egg—all of this against a sky-blue background. As I continued to scrutinize the sheet it looked to me more and more like the many-colored coat of arms that had occurred to me in my dream.

I could not have written Demian even if I had known his address. I decided, however—in the same state of dreamlike presentiment in which I did everything—to send him the painting of the sparrow hawk, even if it would never reach him. I added no message, not even my name, carefully trimmed the edges and wrote my friend's former address on it. Then I mailed it.

I had an exam coming up and had to do more work than usual. The teachers had reinstated me in their favor since I had abruptly changed my previously despicable mode of life. Not that I had become an outstanding student, but now neither I nor anyone else gave it any further thought that half a year earlier my expulsion had seemed almost certain.

My father's letters regained some of their old tone, without reproaches or threats. Yet I felt no inclination to explain to him or anyone else how the change within me had come about. It was an accident that this transformation coincided with my parents' and teachers' wishes. This change did not bring me into the community of the others, did not make me closer to anyone, but actually made me even lonelier. My reformation seemed to point in the direction of Demian, but even this was a distant fate. I did not know myself, for I was too deeply involved. It had begun with Beatrice, but for some time I had been living in such an unreal world with my paintings and my thoughts of Demian that I'd forgotten all about her, too. I could not have uttered a single word about my dreams and expectations, my inner change, to anyone, not even if I had wanted to. But how could I have wanted to?

5) "The Bird Fights Its Way Out of the Egg"

M̲Y̲ ̲P̲A̲I̲N̲T̲E̲D̲ ̲D̲R̲E̲A̲M̲ ̲B̲I̲R̲D̲ was on its way searching for my friend. In what seemed the strangest possible manner a reply reached me.

In my classroom, on my desk, after a break between two lessons I found a note tucked in my book. It was folded exactly the same as notes classmates of mine secretly slipped each other during class. I was only surprised to receive such a note at all, for I had never had that sort of relationship with any student. I thought it would turn out to be an invitation to some prank in which I would not participate anyway—I put the note unread in the front of my book. I came on it again only during the lesson.

Playing with the note I unfolded it carelessly and noticed a few words written on it. One glance was sufficient. One word stopped me cold; in panic I read on while cold fear contracted my heart: "The bird fights its way out of the egg. The egg is the world. Who would be born must first destroy a world. The bird flies to God. That God's name is Abraxas."

After reading over these lines a number of times, I sank into a deep reverie. There could be no doubt about it, this was Demian's reply. No one else could know about my painting. He had grasped its meaning and was helping me interpret it. But how did all of this fit together? And—this oppressed me most of all—what did Abraxas signify? I had never heard nor read the word. "That God's name is Abraxas."

The lesson went on without my taking in a word of it. The next began, the last that morning. It was taught by a young assistant, a Dr. Follens, who had just completed his university studies, whom we liked simply because he was young and unpretentious.

Dr. Follens was guiding us through Herodotus—one of the few subjects that held any interest for me. But today not even Herodotus could hold my attention. I opened the book mechanically but did not follow the translation and remained sunk deep in my own thoughts. Besides, I had frequently confirmed what Demian had told me once during our Confirmation classes: you can achieve anything you desire passionately enough. If I happened to be involved with my own thoughts during a lesson I did not have to worry that the teacher would call on me. If I was distracted or listless, then he would suddenly appear beside me. That had already happened to me. But if I really concentrated, completely wrapped up in a thought of my own, then I was protected. I had also experimented with the trick of staring a person down and had found that it worked. When still with Demian, I had not succeeded in this; now I often felt that a good deal could be accomplished by a sharp glance, and thought.

I was at present nowhere near Herodotus or school. Suddenly the teacher's voice shot like lightning into my consciousness and I awoke terrified. I heard his voice, he practically stood next to me, I even thought he had called my name. But he was not looking at me. I relaxed.

Then I heard his voice again. Loudly it pronounced the word "Abraxas."

In the course of a long explanation, whose beginning I had missed, Dr. Follens went on: "We ought not consider the opinions of those sects and mystical societies as naïve as they appear from the rationalist point of view. Science as we know it today was unknown to antiquity. Instead there existed a preoccupation with philosophical and mystical truths which was highly developed. What grew out of this preoccupation was to some extent merely pedestrian magic and frivolity; perhaps it frequently led to deceptions and crimes, but this magic, too, had noble antecedents in a profound philosophy. As, for instance, the teachings concerning Abraxas which I cited a moment ago. This name occurs in connection with Greek magical formulas and is frequently considered the name of some magician's helper such as certain uncivilized tribes believe in even at present. But it appears that Abraxas has a much deeper significance. We may conceive of the name as that of a godhead whose symbolic task is the uniting of godly and devilish elements."

The learned little man spoke with intelligence and eagerness but no one paid much attention, and as the name Abraxas did not recur, my thoughts turned back to my own affairs.

"Uniting of godly and devilish elements" resounded within me. Here was something for my thoughts to cling to. This idea was familiar to me from conversations with Demian. During the last period of our friendship he had said that we had been given a god to worship who represented only one arbitrarily separated half of the world (it was the official, sanctioned, luminous world), but that we ought to be able to worship the whole world; this meant that we would either have to have a god who was also a devil or institute a cult of the devil alongside the cult of god. And now Abraxas was the god who was both god and devil.

For a time I pursued this thought eagerly but without making any headway. I even pored over a whole libraryful of books seeking a mention of Abraxas. However, my nature had never been disposed to this kind of direct and conscious investigation where at first one finds only truths that are so much dead weight in one's hand.

The figure of Beatrice with which I had occupied myself so intimately and fervently gradually became submerged or, rather, was slowly receding, approaching the horizon more and more, becoming more shadowy and remote, paler. She no longer satisfied the longings of my soul.

In the peculiar self-made isolation in which I existed like a sleepwalker, a new growth began to take shape within me. The longing for life grew—or rather the longing for love. My sexual drive, which I had sublimated for a time in the veneration of Beatrice, demanded new images and objects. But my desires remained unfulfilled and it was more impossible than ever for me to deceive my longings and hope for something from the women with whom my comrades tried their luck. I dreamed vividly again, more in fact by day than at night. Images, pictures, desires arose freely within me, drew me away from the outside world so that I had a more substantial and livelier relationship with the world of my own creation, with these images and dreams and shadows, than with the actual world around me.

A certain dream, or fantasy, that kept recurring gained in meaning for me. The dream, the most important and enduringly significant of my life, went something like this: I was returning to my father's house—above the entrance glowed the heraldic bird, yellow on a blue background; in the house itself my mother was coming toward me—but as I entered and wanted to embrace her, it was not she but a form I had never set eyes on before, tall and strong, resembling Max Demian and the picture I had painted; yet different, for despite its strength it was completely feminine. This form drew me to itself and enveloped me in a deep, tremulous embrace. I felt a mixture of ecstasy and horror—the embrace was at once an act of divine worship and a crime. Too many associations with my mother and friend commingled with this figure embracing me. Its embrace violated all sense of reverence, yet it was bliss. Sometimes I awoke from this dream with a feeling of profound ecstasy, at others in mortal fear and with a racked conscience as though I had committed some terrible crime.

Only gradually and unconsciously did this very intimate image become linked with the hint about the God I was to search for, the hint that had come to me from the outside. The link grew closer and more intimate and I began to sense that I was calling on Abraxas particularly in this dreamed presentiment. Delight and horror, man and woman commingled, the holiest and most shocking were intertwined, deep guilt flashing through most delicate innocence: that was the appearance of my love-dream image and Abraxas, too. Love had ceased to be the dark animalistic drive I had experienced at first with fright, nor was it any longer the devout transfiguration I had offered to Beatrice. It was both, and yet much more. It was the image of an angel and Satan, man and woman in one flesh, man and beast, the highest good and the worst evil. It seemed that I was destined to live in this fashion, this seemed my preordained fate. I yearned for it but feared it at the same time. It was ever-present, hovering constantly above me.

The following spring I was to leave the preparatory school and enter a university. I was still undecided, however, as to where and what I was to study. I had grown a thin mustache, I was a full-grown man, and yet I was completely helpless and without a goal in life. Only one thing was certain: the voice within me, the dream image. I felt the duty to follow this voice blindly wherever it might lead me. But it was difficult and each day I rebelled against it anew. Perhaps I was mad, as I thought at moments; perhaps I was not like other men? But I was able to do the same things the others did; with a little effort and industry I could read Plato, was able to solve problems in trigonometry or follow a chemical analysis. There was only one thing I could not do: wrest the dark secret goal from myself and keep it before me as others did who knew exactly what they wanted to be—professors, lawyers, doctors, artists, however long this would take them and whatever difficulties and advantages this decision would bear in its wake. This I could not do. Perhaps I would become something similar, but how was I to know? Perhaps I would have to continue my search for years on end and would not become anything, and would not reach a goal. Perhaps I would reach this goal but it would turn out to be an evil, dangerous, horrible one?

I wanted only to try to live in accord with the promptings which came from my true self. Why was that so very difficult?

I made frequent attempts to paint the mighty love apparition of my dream. I never succeeded. If I had I would have sent the painting to Demian. Where he was I had no idea. I only knew that we were linked. When would we meet again?

The tranquillity of the weeks and months of my Beatrice period had long since passed. At that time I felt I had reached a safe harbor, an island of peace. But as always, as soon as I had become accustomed to my condition, as soon as a dream had given me hope, it wilted and became useless. It was futile to sorrow after the loss. I now lived within a fire of unsatisfied longing, of tense expectancy that often drove me completely wild. I often saw the beloved apparition of my dream with a clarity greater than life, more distinct than my own hand, spoke with it, wept before it, cursed it. I called it mother and knelt down in front of it in tears. I called it my beloved and had a premonition of its ripe all-fulfilling kiss. I called it devil and whore, vampire and murderer. It enticed me to the gentlest love-dreams and to devastating shamelessness, nothing was too good and precious, nothing was too wicked and low for it.

I experienced the whole of that winter as one unending

inner turbulence, which I find difficult to describe. I had long since become used to my loneliness—that did not oppress me: I lived with Demian, the sparrow hawk, with the mighty apparition of my dream that was both my fate and my beloved. This was enough to sustain me, for everything pointed toward vastness and space—it all pointed toward Abraxas. But none of these dreams, none of these thoughts obeyed me, none were at my beck and call, I could color none of them as I pleased. They came and took me, I was ruled by them, was their vessel.

However, I was well armed against the outside world. I was no longer afraid of people; even my fellow students had come to know this and treated me with a secret respect that often brought a smile to my lips. If I wanted to I could see through most of them and startled them occasionally. Only I rarely or never tried. I was always preoccupied with myself. And I longed desperately to really live for once, to give something of myself to the world, to enter into a relationship and battle with it. Sometimes when I ran through the streets in the evening, unable to return before midnight because I was so restless, I felt that now at this very moment I would have to meet my beloved—as she walked past me at the next street corner, called to me from the nearest window. At other times all of this seemed unbearably painful and I was prepared to commit suicide.

Just then I found a strange refuge—"by chance," as they say—though I believe there is no such thing. If you need something desperately and find it, this is not an accident; your own craving and compulsion leads you to it.

Twice or three times during my walks I had heard

organ music coming from a small church at the edge of town. I had not stopped to listen. The next time I passed this church I heard the music again and recognized Bach. I went to the door, found it locked, and because the street was almost deserted I sat down on a curbstone next to the church, turned up my coat collar, and listened. It was not a big organ but it had good tone. It was being played with a strange, highly personal expression of purpose and tenacity that gave the impression of prayer. I felt that the organist knew the treasures hidden in the music, that he was wooing, hammering at the gate, wrestling for this treasure as for his life. My knowledge of music is technically very limited but from childhood on I have had an intuitive grasp, have sensed music as something self-evident within me.

The organist also played something more modern—it could have been Max Reger. The church was almost completely dark, only a very thin beam of light penetrated the window closest to me. I waited until the music ceased and then paced back and forth until I saw the organist leave the church. He was still young, though older than I, square-shouldered and squat, and he moved off rapidly with vigorous yet seemingly reluctant strides.

From then on I occasionally sat outside the church or paced up and down before it during the evening hours. Once I even found the door open and sat for half an hour in a pew, shivering against the cold, yet happy as long as the organist played in the loft. I not only distinguished his personality in the music he played—every piece he performed also had affinity with the next, a secret connection. Everything he played was full of faith, surrender, and devotion. Yet not devout after the fashion of churchgoers and pastors, devout the way pilgrims and mendicants were in the Middle Ages, devout with that unconditional surrender to a universal feeling that transcends all confessions. He also played music composed prior to Bach, and the old Italians. And all this music said the same thing, all of it expressed what was in the musician's soul: longing, a most intimate atonement with the world and a violent wrenching loose, a burning hearkening to one's own dark soul, an intoxicating surrender and deep curiosity about the miraculous.

Once when I shadowed the organist after he left the church, I saw him enter a small tavern on the edge of town. I could not resist following him in. For the first time I could see him clearly. He sat at a table in the far corner of the small room. He wore a black felt hat. A jug of wine stood before him. His face looked as I suspected it would. He was ugly and a little wild, inquisitive and pigheaded, capricious and determined, yet his mouth had a soft childlike quality. All his masculinity and strength were concentrated in eyes and forehead, while the lower part of the face was sensitive and immature, uncontrolled and somehow very soft. The irresolute, boyish chin appeared to contradict the forehead and eyes—which I liked, those dark-brown eyes, full of pride and hostility.

I sat down opposite him without saying a word. We were the only two guests in the tavern. He gave me a look as though he wanted to shoo me away. But I did not budge, and stared back unmoved until he grumbled morosely: "What on earth are you staring at? Is there something you want?"

"No, I don't want anything from you," I said. "You've given me a great deal already."

He knitted his brows.

"So, you're a music lover. I find it nauseating to be crazy about music."

I did not let him intimidate me.

"I have listened to you often, back there in the church," I said. "But I don't want to trouble you. I thought I might find something, something special; I really don't know what. But don't pay any attention to me. I can listen to you in church."

"But I always lock it."

"Not very long ago you forgot and I sat inside. Usually I stand outside or sit on the curb."

"Really? Next time you can come inside, it's warmer. All you have to do is knock at the door. But you have to bang hard and not while I'm playing. Go ahead now—what did you want to tell me? You're quite young yet, probably a student of some sort. Are you a musician?"

"No. I like listening to music, but only the kind you play, completely unreserved music, the kind that makes you feel that a man is shaking heaven and hell. I believe I love that kind of music because it is amoral. Everything else is so moral that I'm looking for something that isn't. Morality has always seemed to me insufferable. I can't express it very well.—Do you know that there must be a god who is both god and devil at one and the same time? There is supposed to have been one once. I heard about it."

The musician pushed his wide hat back a little and shook the hair out of his eyes, all the while peering at me. He lowered his face across the table.

Softly and expectantly he asked: "What's the name of the god you mentioned?"

"Unfortunately I know next to nothing about him, actually only his name. He is called Abraxas."

The musician blinked suspiciously around him as though someone might be eavesdropping. Then he moved closer to me and said in a whisper: "That's what I thought. Who are you?"

"A student at the prep school."

"How did you happen to hear about Abraxas?"

"By accident."

He struck the table so that wine spilled out of his glass. "By accident! Don't talk *shit*, young fellow! One doesn't hear about Abraxas by accident, and don't you forget it. I will tell you more about him. I know a little."

He fell silent and moved his chair back. When I looked at him full of expectation, he made a face.

"Not here. Some other time. There, take these."

He reached in his coat, which he had not taken off, and drew out a few roasted chestnuts and threw them to me.

I said nothing, took them, ate and felt content.

"All right," he whispered after a moment. "Where did you find out about—Him?"

I did not hesitate to tell him.

"I was alone and desperate at one time," I began. "Then I remembered a friend I had had several years back who I felt knew much more than I did. I had painted something, a bird struggling out of the globe. I sent him this painting. After a time I found a piece of paper with the following words written on it: 'The bird fights its way out of the egg. The egg is the world. Who would be born must first destroy a world. The bird flies to God. That God's name is Abraxas.' "

He made no reply. We shelled our chestnuts and drank
our wine.

"Another glass?" he asked.

"No, thanks. I don't like drinking."

He laughed, a little disappointed.

"As you like. It's different with me. I'll stay but you can
run along if you want."

When I joined him the next time, after he had played
the organ, he was not very communicative. He led me
down an alley and through an old and impressive house
and up to a large, somewhat dark and neglected room.
Except for a piano, nothing in it gave a hint of his being a
musician—but a large bookcase and a desk gave the room
an almost scholarly air.

"How many books you have!" I exclaimed.

"Part of them are from my father's library—in whose
house I live. Yes, young man, I'm living with my parents
but I can't introduce you to them. My acquaintances
aren't regarded very favorably in this house. I'm the black
sheep. My father is fabulously respectable and an important pastor and preacher in this town. And I, so that you
know the score at once, am his talented and promising
son who has gone astray and, to some extent, even mad. I
was a theology student but shortly before my state exams
I left this very respectable department; that is, not entirely, not in so far as it concerns my private studies, for
I'm still most interested to see what kinds of gods people
have devised for themselves. Otherwise, I'm a musician at
present and it looks as though I will receive a small post
as an organist somewhere. Then I'll be back in the employ
of the church again."

As much as the feeble light from the small table lamp

permitted, I glanced along the spines of the books and noticed Greek, Latin, and Hebrew titles. Meanwhile my acquaintance had lain down on the floor and was busying himself with something.

"Come," he called after a moment, "we want to practice a bit of philosophy. That means: keep your mouth shut, lie on your stomach, and meditate."

He struck a match and lit paper and wood in the fireplace in front of which he sprawled. The flames leapt high, he stirred and fed them with the greatest care. I lay down beside him on the worn-out carpet. For about an hour we lay on our stomachs silent before the shimmering wood, watching the flames shoot up and roar, sink down and double over, flicker and twitch, and in the end brood quietly on sunken embers.

"Fire worship was by no means the most foolish thing ever invented," he murmured to himself at one point. Otherwise neither of us said a word. I stared fixedly into the flames, lost myself in dreams and stillness, recognized figures in the smoke and pictures in the ashes. Once I was startled. My companion threw a piece of resin into the embers: a slim flame shot up and I recognized the bird with the yellow sparrow hawk's head. In the dying embers, red and gold threads ran together into nets, letters of the alphabet appeared, memories of faces, animals, plants, worms, and snakes. As I emerged from my reveries I looked at my companion, his chin resting on his fists, staring fanatically into the ashes with complete surrender.

"I have to go now," I said softly.

"Go ahead then. Good-by."

He did not get up. The lamp had gone out: I groped my way through the dark rooms and hallways of the bewitched old house. Once outside, I stopped and looked up along its façade. Every window was dark. A small brass plate on the front door gleamed in the light from a street lamp. On it I read the words: "Pistorius, pastor primarius."

Not until I was at home and sat in my little room after supper did it occur to me that I had not heard anything about either Abraxas or Pistorius—we'd exchanged hardly a dozen words. But I was very satisfied with my visit. And for our next meeting he had promised to play an exquisite piece of old music, an organ passacaglia by Buxtehude.

Without my being entirely aware of it, the organist Pistorius had given me my first lesson when we were sprawled on the floor before the fire in his depressing hermit's room. Staring into the blaze had been a tonic for me, confirming tendencies that I had always had but never cultivated. Gradually some of them were becoming comprehensible to me.

Even as a young boy I had been in the habit of gazing at bizarre natural phenomena, not so much observing them as surrendering to their magic, their confused, deep language. Long gnarled tree roots, colored veins in rocks, patches of oil floating on water, light-refracting flaws in glass—all these things had held great magic for me at one time: water and fire particularly, smoke, clouds, and dust, but most of all the swirling specks of color that swam before my eyes the minute I closed them. I began to remember all this in the days after my visit to Pistorius, for I noticed that a certain strength and joy, an intensification of my self-awareness that I had felt since that evening, I owed exclusively to this prolonged staring into the fire. It was remarkably comforting and rewarding.

To the few experiences which helped me along the way toward my life's true goal I added this new one: the observation of such configurations. The surrender to Nature's irrational, strangely confused formations produces in us a feeling of inner harmony with the force responsible for these phenomena. We soon fall prey to the temptation of thinking of them as being our own moods, our own creations, and see the boundaries separating us from Nature begin to quiver and dissolve. We become acquainted with that state of mind in which we are unable to decide whether the images on our retina are the result of impressions coming from without or from within. Nowhere as in this exercise can we discover so easily and simply to what extent we are creative, to what extent our soul partakes of the constant creation of the world. For it is the same indivisible divinity that is active through us and in Nature, and if the outside world were to be destroyed, a single one of us would be capable of rebuilding it: mountain and stream, tree and leaf, root and flower, yes, every natural form is latent within us, originates in the soul whose essence is eternity, whose essence we cannot know but which most often intimates itself to us as the power to love and create.

Not until many years later did I find these observations of mine confirmed, in a book by Leonardo da Vinci, who describes at one point how good, how intensely interesting it is to look at a wall many people have spit on. Confronted with each stain on the wet wall, he must have felt the same as Pistorius and I felt before the fire.

The next time we were together, the organist gave me an explanation: "We always define the limits of our personality too narrowly. In general, we count as part of our personality only that which we can recognize as being an individual trait or as diverging from the norm. But we consist of everything the world consists of, each of us, and just as our body contains the genealogical table of evolution as far back as the fish and even much further, so we bear everything in our soul that once was alive in the soul of men. Every god and devil that ever existed, be it among the Greeks, Chinese, or Zulus, are within us, exist as latent possibilities, as wishes, as alternatives. If the human race were to vanish from the face of the earth save for one halfway talented child that had received no education, this child would rediscover the entire course of evolution, it would be capable of producing everything once more, gods and demons, paradises, commandments, the Old and New Testament."

"Yes, fine," I replied. "But what is the value of the individual in that case? Why do we continue striving if everything has been completed within us?"

"Stop!" exclaimed Pistorius. "There's an immense difference between simply carrying the world within us and being aware of it. A madman can spout ideas that remind you of Plato, and a pious little seminary student rethinks deep mythological correspondences found among the Gnostics or in Zoroaster. But he isn't aware of them. He is a tree or stone, at best an animal, as long as he is not conscious. But as soon as the first spark of recognition dawns within him he is a human being. You wouldn't consider all the bipeds you pass on the street human beings simply because they walk upright and carry their young in their bellies nine months! It is obvious how many of them are fish or sheep, worms or angels, how many are ants, how many are bees! Well, each one of them contains the possibility of becoming human, but only by having an intimation of these possibilities, partially even by learning to make himself conscious of them; only in this respect are these possibilities his."

This was the general drift of our conversations. They rarely confronted me with anything completely new, anything altogether astonishing. But everything, even the most ordinary matters, resembled gentle persistent hammer blows on the same spot within me; all of them helped me to form myself, all of them helped to peel off layers of skin, to break eggshells, and after each blow I lifted my head a little higher, a little more freely, until my yellow bird pushed its beautiful raptor's head out of the shattered shell of the terrestial globe.

Frequently we also told each other our dreams. Pistorius knew how to interpret them. An example of this comes to mind just now. I dreamed I was able to fly, but in such a way that I seemed catapulted into the air and lost all control. The feeling of flying exhilarated me, but exhilaration turned to fear when I saw myself driven higher and higher, becoming more and more powerless. At that instant I made the saving discovery that I could regulate the rise or fall of my flight by holding or releasing my breath.

Pistorius' comment was: "The impetus that makes you fly is our great human possession. Everybody has it. It is the feeling of being linked with the roots of power, but one soon becomes afraid of this feeling. It's damned dangerous! That is why most people shed their wings and prefer to walk and obey the law. But not you. You go on flying. And look! You discover that you gradually begin to master your flight, that to the great general force that tears you upward there is added a delicate, small force of your own, an organ, a steering mechanism. How marvelous! Lacking that, you would be drawn up to the heights, powerless—which is what happens to madmen. They possess deeper intimations than people who remain earthbound, but they have no key and no steering mechanism and roar off into infinity. But you, Sinclair, you are going about it the right way. How? You probably don't know yourself. You are doing it with a new organ, with something that regulates your breathing. And now you will realize how little 'individuality' your soul has in its deepest reaches. For it does not invent this regulator! It is not new! You've borrowed it: it has existed for thousands of years. It is the organ with which fish regulate their equilibrium—the air bladder. And in fact among the fish there are still a few strange primeval genera where the air bladder functions as a kind of lung and can be used on occasion as a breathing mechanism. In other words, exactly like the lung which you in your dream use as a flying bladder."

He even brought out a zoology book and showed me the names and illustrations of these anachronistic fish. And with a peculiar shudder I felt that an organ from an earlier period of evolution was still alive within me.

6)   Jacob Wrestling

IT IS IMPOSSIBLE to recount briefly all that Pistorius the eccentric musician told me about Abraxas. Most important was that what I learned from him represented a further step on the road toward myself. At that time, I was an unusual young man of eighteen, precocious in a hundred ways, in a hundred others immature and helpless. When I compared myself with other boys my age I often felt proud and conceited but just as often humiliated and depressed. Frequently I considered myself a genius, and just as frequently, crazy. I did not succeed in participating in the life of boys my age, was often consumed by self-reproach and worries: I was helplessly separated from them, I was debarred from life.

Pistorius, who was himself a full-grown eccentric, taught me to maintain my courage and self-respect. By always finding something of value in what I said, in my dreams, my fantasies and thoughts, by never making light of them, always giving them serious consideration, he became my model.

"You told me," he said, "that you love music because it is *amoral*. That's all right with me. But in that case you can't allow yourself to be a moralist either. You can't compare yourself with others: if Nature has made you a bat you shouldn't try to be an ostrich. You consider yourself odd at times, you accuse yourself of taking a road different from most people. You have to unlearn that. Gaze into the fire, into the clouds, and as soon as the inner voices begin to speak, surrender to them, don't ask first whether it's permitted or would please your teachers or father, or some god. You will ruin yourself if you do that. That way you will become earthbound, a vegetable. Sinclair, our god's name is Abraxas and he is God and Satan and he contains both the luminous and the dark world. Abraxas does not take exception to any of your thoughts, any of your dreams. Never forget that. But he will leave you once you've become blameless and normal. Then he will leave you and look for a different vessel in which to brew his thoughts."

Among all my dreams the dark dream of love was the most faithful. How often I dreamed that I stepped beneath the heraldic bird into our house, wanted to draw my mother to me and instead held the great, half-male, half-maternal woman in my arms, of whom I was afraid but who also attracted me violently. And I could never confess this dream to my friend. I kept it to myself even after I had told him everything else. It was my corner, my secret, my refuge.

When I felt bad I asked Pistorius to play Buxtehude's passacaglia. Then I would sit in the dusk-filled church completely involved in this unusually intimate, self-absorbed music, music that seemed to listen to itself, that comforted me each time, prepared me more and more to heed my own inner voices.

At times we stayed even after the music had ceased: we watched the weak light filter through the high, sharply arched windows and lose itself in the church.

"It sounds odd," said Pistorius, "that I was a theology student once and almost became a pastor. But I only committed a mistake of form. My task and goal still is to be a priest. Yet I was satisfied too soon and offered myself to Jehovah before I knew about Abraxas. Oh, yes, each and every religion is beautiful; religion is soul, no matter whether you take part in Christian communion or make a pilgrimage to Mecca."

"But in that case," I intervened, "you actually could have become a pastor."

"No, Sinclair. I would have had to lie. Our religion is practiced as though it were something else, something totally ineffectual. If worst came to worst I might become a Catholic, but a Protestant pastor—no! The few genuine believers—I do know a few—prefer the literal interpretation. I would not be able to tell them, for example, that Christ is not a person for me but a hero, a myth, an extraordinary shadow image in which humanity has painted itself on the wall of eternity. And the others, that come to church to hear a few clever phrases, to fulfill an obligation, not to miss anything, and so forth, what should I have said to them? Convert them? Is that what you mean? But I have no desire to. A priest does not want to convert, he merely wants to live among believers, among his own kind. He wants to be the instrument and expression for the feeling from which we create our gods."

He interrupted himself. Then continued: "My friend,

our new religion, for which we have chosen the name Abraxas, is beautiful. It is the best we have. But it is still a fledgling. Its wings haven't grown yet. A lonely religion isn't right either. There has to be a community, there must be a cult and intoxicants, feasts and mysteries . . ."

He sank into a reverie and became lost within himself.

"Can't one perform mysteries all by oneself or among a very small group?" I asked hesitantly.

"Yes, one can." He nodded. "I've been performing them for a long time by myself. I have cults of my own for which I would be sentenced to years in prison if anyone should ever find out about them. Still, I know that it's not the right thing either."

Suddenly he slapped me on the shoulder so that I started up. "Boy," he said intensely, "you, too, have mysteries of your own. I know that you must have dreams that you don't tell me. I don't want to know them. But I can tell you: live those dreams, play with them, build altars to them. It is not yet the ideal but it points in the right direction. Whether you and I and a few others will renew the world someday remains to be seen. But within ourselves we must renew it each day, otherwise we just aren't serious. Don't forget that! You are eighteen years old, Sinclair, you don't go running to prostitutes. You must have dreams of love, you must have desires. Perhaps you're made in such a way that you are afraid of them. Don't be. They are the best things you have. You can believe me. I lost a great deal when I was your age by violating those dreams of love. One shouldn't do that. When you know something about Abraxas, you cannot do this any longer. You aren't allowed to be afraid of anything, you can't consider prohibited anything that the soul desires."

Startled, I countered: "But you can't do everything that comes to your mind! You can't kill someone because you detest him."

He moved closer to me.

"Under certain circumstances, even that. Yet it is a mistake most of the time. I don't mean that you should simply do everything that pops into your head. No. But you shouldn't harm and drive away those ideas that make good sense by exorcising them or moralizing about them. Instead of crucifying yourself or someone else you can drink wine from a chalice and contemplate the mystery of the sacrifice. Even without such procedures you can treat your drives and so-called temptations with respect and love. Then they will reveal their meaning—and they all do have meaning. If you happen to think of something truly mad or sinful again, if you want to kill someone or want to commit some enormity, Sinclair, think at that moment that it is Abraxas fantasizing within you! The person whom you would like to do away with is of course never Mr. X but merely a disguise. If you hate a person, you hate something in him that is part of yourself. What isn't part of ourselves doesn't disturb us."

Never before had Pistorius said anything to me that had touched me as deeply as this. I could not reply. But what had affected me most and in the strangest way was the similarity of this exhortation to Demian's words, which I had been carrying around with me for years. They did not know each other, yet both of them had told me the same thing.

"The things we see," Pistorius said softly, "are the same

things that are within us. There is no reality except the
one contained within us. That is why so many people live
such an unreal life. They take the images outside them for
reality and never allow the world within to assert itself.
You can be happy that way. But once you know the other
interpretation you no longer have the choice of following
the crowd. Sinclair, the majority's path is an easy one,
ours is difficult."

A few days later, after I had twice waited in vain, I met
him late at night as he came seemingly blown around a
corner by the cold night wind, stumbling all over himself,
dead drunk. I felt no wish to call him. He went past me
without seeing me, staring in front of himself with bewildered eyes shining, as though he followed something
darkly calling out of the unknown. I followed him the
length of one street; he drifted along as though pulled by
an invisible string, with a fanatic gait, yet loose, like a
ghost. Sadly I returned home to my unfulfilled dreams.

So that is how he renews the world within himself! it
occurred to me. At the same moment I felt that was a low,
moralizing thought. What did I know of his dreams? Perhaps he walked a more certain path in his intoxication
than I within my dream.

I had noticed a few times during the breaks between
classes that a fellow student I had never paid any previous attention to seemed to seek me out. He was a delicate, weak-looking boy with thin red-blond hair, and the
look in his eyes and his behavior seemed unusual. One
evening when I was coming home he was lying in wait for
me in the alley. He let me walk past, then followed me and
stopped when I did before the front door.

"Is there something you want from me?" I asked him.

"I would only like to talk with you once," he said shyly. "Be so kind as to walk with me for a moment."

I followed him, sensing that he was excited and full of expectation. His hands trembled.

"Are you a spiritualist?" he asked suddenly.

"No, Knauer," I said laughing. "Not in the least. What makes you think I am?"

"But then you must be a theosophist?"

"Neither."

"Oh, don't be so reticent! I can feel there's something special about you. There's a look in your eyes . . . I'm positive you communicate with spirits. I'm not asking out of idle curiosity, Sinclair. No, I am a seeker myself, you know, and I'm so very alone."

"Go ahead, tell me about it," I encouraged him. "I don't know much about spirits. I live in my dreams—that's what you sense. Other people live in dreams, but not in their own. That's the difference."

"Yes, maybe that's the way it is," he whispered. "It doesn't matter what kinds of dreams they are in which you live.—Have you heard about white magic?"

I had to say no.

"That is when you learn self-control. You can become immortal and bewitch people. Have you ever practiced any exercises?"

After I had inquired what these "exercises" were he became very secretive; that is, until I turned to go back. Then he told me everything.

"For instance, when I want to fall asleep or want to concentrate on something I do one of these exercises. I think of something, a word for example, or a name or a geometrical form. Then I think this form into myself as hard as I can. I try to imagine it until I can actually feel it inside my head. Then I think it in the throat, and so forth, until I am completely filled by it. Then I'm as firm as though I had turned to stone and nothing can distract me any more."

I had a vague idea of what he meant. Yet I felt certain that there was something else troubling him, he was so strangely excited and restless. I tried to make it easy for him to speak, and it was not long before he expressed his real concern.

"You're continent, too, aren't you?" he asked reluctantly.

"What do you mean, sexually?"

"Yes. I've been continent for two years—ever since I found out about the exercises. I had been depraved until then, you know what I mean.—So you've never been with a woman?"

"No," I said. "I never found the right one."

"But if you did find a woman that you felt was the right one, would you sleep with Her?"

"Yes, naturally—if she had no objections," I said a little derisively.

"Oh, you're on the wrong path altogether! You can train your inner powers only if you're completely continent. I've been—for two whole years. Two years and a little more than a month! It's so difficult! Sometimes I think I can't stand it much longer."

"Listen, Knauer, I don't believe that continence is all that important."

"I know," he objected. "That's what they all say. But I didn't expect you to say the same thing. If you want to take the higher, the spiritual road you have to remain absolutely pure."

"Well, be pure then! But I don't understand why someone is supposed to be more pure than another person if he suppresses his sexual urges. Or are you capable of eliminating sex from all your thoughts and dreams?"

He looked at me despairingly.

"No, that's just the point. My God, but I have to. I have dreams at night that I couldn't even tell myself. Horrible dreams."

I remembered what Pistorius had told me. But much as I agreed with his ideas I could not pass them on. I was incapable of giving advice that did not derive from my own experience and which I myself did not have the strength to follow. I fell silent and felt humiliated at being unable to give advice to someone who was seeking it from me.

"I've tried everything!" moaned Knauer beside me. "I've done everything there is to do. Cold water, snow, physical exercise and running, but nothing helps. Each night I awake from dreams that I'm not even allowed to think about—and the horrible part is that in the process I'm gradually forgetting everything spiritual I ever learned. I hardly ever succeed any more in concentrating or in making myself fall asleep. Often I lie awake the whole night. It can't go on much longer like this. If I can't win the struggle, if in the end I give in and become impure again, I'll be more wicked than all the others who never put up a fight. You understand that, don't you?"

I nodded but was unable to make any comment. He began to bore me and I was startled that his evident need and despair made no deeper impression on me. My only feeling was: I can't help you.

"So you don't know anything?" he finally asked sadly and exhausted. "Nothing at all? But there must be a way. How do you do it?"

"I can't tell you anything, Knauer. We can't help anybody else. No one helped me either. You have to come to terms with yourself and then you must do what your inmost heart desires. There is no other way. If you can't find it yourself you'll find no spirits either."

The little fellow looked at me, disappointed and suddenly bereft of speech. Then his eyes flashed with hatred, he grimaced and shrieked: "Ah, you're a fine saint! You're depraved yourself, I know. You pretend to be wise but secretly you cling to the same filth the rest of us do! You're a pig, a pig, like me. All of us are pigs!"

I went off and left him standing there. He followed me two or three steps, then turned around and ran away. I felt nauseated with pity and disgust and the feeling did not leave me until I had surrounded myself with several paintings back in my room and surrendered to my own dreams. Instantly the dream returned, of the house entrance and the coat of arms, of the mother and the strange woman, and I could see her features so distinctly that I began painting her picture that same evening.

When the painting was completed after several days' work, sketched out in dreamlike fifteen-minute spurts, I pinned it on the wall, moved the study lamp in front of it, and stood before it as though before a ghost with which I had had to struggle to the end. It was a face similar to the earlier one—a few features even resembled me. One eye was noticeably higher than the other and the gaze went over and beyond me, self-absorbed and rigid, full of fate.

I stood before it and began to freeze inside from the exertion. I questioned the painting, berated it, made love to it, prayed to it; I called it mother, called it whore and slut, called it my beloved, called it Abraxas. Words said by Pistorius—or Demian?—occurred to me between my imprecations. I could not remember who had said them but I felt I could hear them again. They were words about Jacob's wrestling with the angel of God and his "I will not let thee go except thou bless me."

The painted face in the lamplight changed with each exhortation—became light and luminous, dark and brooding, closed pale eyelids over dead eyes, opened them again and flashed lightning glances. It was woman, man, girl, a little child, an animal, it dissolved into a tiny patch of color, grew large and distinct again. Finally, following a strong impulse, I closed my eyes and now saw the picture within me, stronger and mightier than before. I wanted to kneel down before it but it was so much a part of me that I could not separate it from myself, as though it had been transformed into my own ego.

Then I heard a dark, heavy roaring as if just before a spring storm and I trembled with an indescribable new feeling of fearful experience. Stars flashed up before me and died away: memories as far back as my earliest forgotten childhood, yes, even as far back as my pre-existence at earlier stages of evolution, thronged past me. But these memories that seemed to repeat every secret of my life to me did not stop with the past and the present. They went beyond it, mirroring the future, tore me away from the present into new forms of life whose images shone blindingly clear—not one could I clearly remember later on.

During the night I awoke from deep sleep: still dressed I lay diagonally across the bed. I lit the lamp, felt that I had to recollect something important but could not remember anything about the previous hour. Gradually I began to have an inkling. I looked for the painting—it was no longer on the wall, nor on the table either. Then I thought I could dimly remember that I had burned it. Or had this been in my dream that I burned it in the palm of my hand and swallowed the ashes?

A great restlessness overcame me. I put on a hat and walked out of the house through the alley as though compelled, ran through innumerable streets and squares as though driven by a frenzy, listened briefly in front of my friend's dark church, searched, searched with extreme urgency—without knowing what. I walked through a quarter with brothels where I could still see here and there a lighted window. Farther on I reached an area of newly built houses, with piles of bricks everywhere partially covered with gray snow. I remembered—as I drifted under the sway of some strange compulsion like a sleepwalker through the streets—the new building back in my home town to which my tormentor Kromer had taken me for my first payment. A similar building stood before me now in the gray night, its dark entrance yawning at me. It drew me inside: wanting to escape I stumbled over sand and rubbish. The power that drove me was stronger: I was forced to enter.

Across boards and bricks I stumbled into a dreary room that smelled moist and cold from fresh cement. There was a pile of sand, a light-gray patch, otherwise it was dark.

Then a horrified voice called out: "My God, Sinclair, where did you come from?"

Beside me a figure rose up out of the darkness, a small lean fellow, like a ghost, and even in my terror I recognized my fellow student Knauer.

"How did you happen to come here?" he asked, mad with excitement. "How were you able to find me?"

I didn't understand.

"I wasn't looking for you," I said, benumbed. Each word meant a great effort and came only haltingly, through dead lips.

He stared at me.

"Weren't looking for me?"

"No. Something drew me. Did you call me? You must have called me. What are you doing here anyway? It's night."

He clasped me convulsively with his thin arms.

"Yes, night. Morning will soon be here. Can you forgive me?"

"Forgive you what?"

"Oh, I was so awful."

Only now I remembered our conversation. Had that been only four, five days ago? A whole lifetime seemed to have passed since then. But suddenly I knew everything. Not only what had transpired between us but also why I had come here and what Knauer had wanted to do out here.

"You wanted to commit suicide, Knauer?"

He trembled with cold and fear.

"Yes, I wanted to. I don't know whether I would have been able to. I wanted to wait until morning."

I drew him into the open. The first horizontal rays of

daylight glimmered cold and listless in the gray dawn.

For a while I led the boy by the arm. I heard myself say: "Now go home and don't say a word to anyone! You were on the wrong path. We aren't pigs as you seem to think, but human beings. We create gods and struggle with them, and they bless us."

We walked on and parted company without saying another word. When I reached the house, it was already daylight.

The best things I gained from my remaining weeks in St. —————— were the hours spent with Pistorius at the organ or in front of his fire. We were studying a Greek text about Abraxas and he read me extracts from a translation of the Vedas and taught me how to speak the sacred "om." Yet these occult matters were not what nourished me inwardly. What invigorated me was the progress I had made in discovering my self, the increasing confidence in my own dreams, thoughts, and intimations, and the growing knowledge of the power I possessed within me.

Pistorius and I understood each other in every possible way. All I had to do was think of him and I could be certain that he—or a message from him—would come. I could ask him anything, as I had asked Demian, without his having to be present in the flesh: all I had to do was visualize him and direct my questions at him in the form of intensive thought. Then all psychic effort expended on the question would return to me in kind, as an answer. Only it was not the person of Pistorius nor that of Max Demian that I conjured up and addressed, but the picture I had dreamed and painted, the half-male, half-female dream image of my *daemon.* This being was now no

longer confined to my dreams, no longer merely depicted
on paper, but lived within me as an ideal and intensification of my self.

The relationship which the would-be suicide Knauer
formed with me was peculiar, occasionally even funny.
Ever since the night in which I had been sent to him, he
clung to me like a faithful servant or a dog, made every
effort to forge his life with mine, and obeyed me blindly.
He came to me with the most astonishing questions and
requests, wanted to see spirits, learn the cabala, and
would not believe me when I assured him that I was
totally ignorant in all these matters. He thought nothing
was beyond my powers. Yet it was strange that he would
often come to me with his puzzling and stupid questions
when I was faced with a puzzle of my own to which his
fanciful notions and requests frequently provided a catch-
word and the impetus for a solution. Often he was a
bother and I would dismiss him peremptorily; yet I
sensed that he, too, had been sent to me, that from him,
too, came back whatever I gave him, in double measure;
he too, was a leader for me—or at least a guidepost. The
occult books and writings he brought me and in which he
sought his salvation taught me more than I realized at the
time.

Later Knauer slipped unnoticed out of my life. We
never came into conflict with each other; there was no
reason to. Unlike Pistorius, with whom I was still to share
a strange experience toward the end of my days in
St. ———.

On one or on several occasions in the course of their
lives, even the most harmless people do not altogether
escape coming into conflict with the fine virtues of piety

and gratitude. Sooner or later each of us must take the step that separates him from his father, from his mentors; each of us must have some cruelly lonely experience—even if most people cannot take much of this and soon crawl back. I myself had not parted from my parents and their world, the "luminous" world in a violent struggle, but had gradually and almost imperceptibly become estranged. I was sad that it had to be this way and it made for many unpleasant hours during my visits back home; but it did not affect me deeply, it was bearable.

But where we have given of our love and respect not from habit but of our own free will, where we have been disciples and friends out of our inmost hearts, it is a bitter and horrible moment when we suddenly recognize that the current within us wants to pull us away from what is dearest to us. Then every thought that rejects the friend and mentor turns in our own hearts like a poisoned barb, then each blow struck in defense flies back into one's own face, the words "disloyalty" and "ingratitude" strike the person who feels he was morally sound like catcalls and stigma, and the frightened heart flees timidly back to the charmed valleys of childhood virtues, unable to believe that this break, too, must be made, this bond also broken.

With time my inner feelings had slowly turned against acknowledging Pistorius so unreservedly as a master. My friendship with him, his counsel, the comfort he had brought me, his proximity had been a vital experience during the most important months of my adolescence. God had spoken to me through him. From his lips my dreams had returned clarified and interpreted. He had given me faith in myself. And now I became conscious of gradually beginning to resist him. There was too much didacticism in what he said, and I felt that he understood only a part of me completely.

No quarrel or scene occurred between us, no break and not even a settling of accounts. I uttered only a single— actually harmless—phrase, yet it was in that moment that an illusion was shattered.

A vague presentiment of such an occurrence had oppressed me for some time; it became a distinct feeling one Sunday morning in his study. We were lying before the fire while he was holding forth about mysteries and forms of religion, which he was studying, and whose potentialities for the future preoccupied him. All this seemed to me odd and eclectic and not of vital importance; there was something vaguely pedagogical about it; it sounded like tedious research among the ruins of former worlds. And all at once I felt a repugnance for his whole manner, for this cult of mythologies, this game of mosaics he was playing with secondhand modes of belief.

"Pistorius," I said suddenly in a fit of malice that both surprised and frightened me. "You ought to tell me one of your dreams again sometime, a real dream, one that you've had at night. What you're telling me there is all so—so damned *antiquarian*."

He had never heard me speak like that before and at the same moment I realized with a flash of shame and horror that the arrow I had shot at him, that had pierced his heart, had come from his own armory: I was now flinging back at him reproaches that on occasion he had directed against himself half in irony.

He fell silent at once. I looked at him with dread in my heart and saw him turning terribly pale.

After a long pregnant pause he placed fresh wood on

the fire and said in a quiet voice: "You're right, Sinclair, you're a clever boy. I'll spare you the antiquarian stuff from now on." He spoke very calmly but it was obvious he was hurt. What had I done?

I wanted to say something encouraging to him, implore his forgiveness, assure him of my love and my deep gratitude. Touching words came to mind—but I could not utter them. I just lay there gazing into the fire and kept silent. He, too, kept silent and so we lay while the fire dwindled, and with each dying flame I felt something beautiful, intimate irrevocably burn low and become evanescent.

"I'm afraid you've misunderstood me," I said finally with a very forced and clipped voice. The stupid, meaningless words fell mechanically from my lips as if I were reading from a magazine serial.

"I quite understand," Pistorius said softly. "You're right." I waited. Then he went on slowly: "Inasmuch as one person can be right *against* another."

No, no! I'm wrong, a voice screamed inside me—but I could not say anything. I knew that with my few words I had put my finger on his essential weakness, his affliction and wound. I had touched the spot where he most mistrusted himself. His ideal *was* "antiquarian," he was seeking in the past, he was a romantic. And suddenly I realized deeply within me: what Pistorious had been and given to me was precisely what he could not be and give to himself. He had led me along a path that would transcend and leave even him, the leader, behind.

God knows how one happens to say something like that. I had not meant it all that maliciously, had had no idea of the havoc I would create. I had uttered something the implications of which I had been unaware of at the moment of speaking. I had succumbed to a weak, rather witty but malicious impulse and it had become fate. I had committed a trivial and careless act of brutality which he regarded as a judgment.

How much I wished then that he become enraged, defend himself, and berate me! He did nothing of the kind—I had to do all of that myself. He would have smiled if he could have, and the fact that he found it impossible was the surest proof of how deeply I had wounded him.

By accepting this blow so quietly, from me, his impudent and ungrateful pupil, by keeping silent and admitting that I had been right, by acknowledging my words as his fate, he made me detest myself and increased my indiscretion even more. When I had hit out I had thought I would strike a tough, well-armed man—he turned out to be a quiet, passive, defenseless creature who surrendered without protest.

For a long time we stayed in front of the dying fire, in which each glowing shape, each writhing twig reminded me of our rich hours and increased the guilty awareness of my indebtedness to Pistorius. Finally I could bear it no longer. I got up and left. I stood a long time in front of the door to his room, a long time on the dark stairway, and even longer outside his house waiting to hear if he would follow me. Then I turned to go and walked for hours through the town, its suburbs, parks and woods, until evening. During that walk I felt for the first time the mark of Cain on my forehead.

Only gradually was I able to think clearly about what had occurred. At first my thoughts were full of self-reproach, intent on defending Pistorius. But all of them turned into the opposite of my intention. A thousand times I was ready to regret and take back my rash statement—yet it had been the truth. Only now I managed to understand Pistorius completely and succeeded in constructing his whole dream before me. This dream had been to be a priest, to proclaim the new religion, to introduce new forms of exaltation, of love, of worship, to erect new symbols. But this was not his strength and it was not his function. He lingered too fondly in the past, his knowledge of this past was too precise, he knew too much about Egypt and India, Mithras and Abraxas. His love was shackled to images the earth had seen before, and yet, in his inmost heart, he realized that the New had to be truly new and different, that it had to spring from fresh soil and could not be drawn from museums and libraries. His function was perhaps to lead men to themselves as he had led me. To provide them with the unprecedented, the new gods, was not in him.

At this point a sharp realization burned within me: each man has his "function" but none which he can choose himself, define, or perform as he pleases. It was wrong to desire new gods, completely wrong to want to provide the world with something. An enlightened man had but one duty—to seek the way to himself, to reach inner certainty, to grope his way forward, no matter where it led. The realization shook me profoundly, it was the fruit of this experience. I had often speculated with images of the future, dreamed of roles that I might be assigned, perhaps as poet or prophet or painter, or something similar. All that was futile. I did not exist to write poems, to preach or to paint, neither I nor anyone else. All of that was incidental. Each man had only one genuine vocation —to find the way to himself. He might end up as poet or madman, as prophet or criminal—that was not his affair, ultimately it was of no concern. His task was to discover his own destiny—not an arbitrary one—and live it out wholly and resolutely within himself. Everything else was only a would-be existence, an attempt at evasion, a flight back to the ideals of the masses, conformity and fear of one's own inwardness. The new vision rose up before me, glimpsed a hundred times, possibly even expressed before but now experienced for the first time by me. I was an experiment on the part of Nature, a gamble within the unknown, perhaps for a new purpose, perhaps for nothing, and my only task was to allow this game on the part of primeval depths to take its course, to feel its will within me and make it wholly mine. That or nothing!

I had already felt much loneliness, now there was a deeper loneliness still which was inescapable.

I made no attempt at reconciliation with Pistorius. We remained friends but the relationship changed. Yet this was something we touched on only once; actually it was Pistorius alone who did. He said:

"You know that I have the desire to become a priest. Most of all I wanted to become the priest of the new religion of which you and I have had so many intimations. That role will never be mine—I realize that and even without wholly admitting it to myself have known it for some time. So I will perform other priestly duties instead, perhaps at the organ, perhaps some other way. But I must always have things around me that I feel are beautiful and sacred, organ music and mysteries, symbols and myths. I need and cannot forgo them. That is my weakness. Sometimes, Sinclair, I know that I should not have such wishes, that they are a weakness and luxury. It would be more magnanimous and just if I put myself unreservedly at the disposal of fate. But I can't do that, I am incapable of it. Perhaps you will be able to do it one day. It is difficult, it is the only truly difficult thing there is. I have often dreamed of doing so, but I can't; the idea fills me with dread: I am not capable of standing so naked and alone. I, too, am a poor weak creature who needs warmth and food and occasionally the comfort of human companionship. Someone who seeks nothing but his own fate no longer has any companions, he stands quite alone and has only cold universal space around him. That is Jesus in the Garden of Gethsemane, you know. There have been martyrs who gladly let themselves be nailed to the cross, but even these were no heroes, were not liberated, for even they wanted something that they had become fond of and accustomed to—they had models, they had ideals. But the man who only seeks his destiny has neither models nor ideals, has nothing dear and consoling! And actually this is the path one should follow. People like you and me are quite lonely really but we still have each other, we have the secret satisfaction of being different, of rebelling, of desiring the unusual. But you must shed that, too, if you want to go all the way to the end. You cannot allow yourself to become a revolutionary, an example, a martyr. It is beyond imagining—"

Yes, it was beyond imagining. But it could be dreamed, anticipated, sensed. A few times I had a foretaste of it—in an hour of absolute stillness. Then I would gaze into myself and confront the image of my fate. Its eyes would be full of wisdom, full of madness, they would radiate love or deep malice, it was all the same. You were not allowed to choose or desire any one of them. You were only allowed to desire *yourself*, only your fate. Up to this point, Pistorius had been my guide,

In those days I walked about as though I were blind. I felt frenzies—each step was a new danger. I saw nothing in front of me except the unfathomable darkness into which all paths I had taken until now had led and vanished. And within me I saw the image of the master, who resembled Demian, and in whose eyes my fate stood written.

I wrote on a piece of paper: "A leader has left me. I am enveloped in darkness. I cannot take another step alone. Help me."

I wanted to mail it to Demian, but didn't. Each time I wanted to, it looked foolish and senseless. But I knew my little prayer by heart and often recited it to myself. It was with me every hour of the day. I had begun to understand it.

My schooldays were over. I was to take a trip during my vacation—my father's idea—and then enter a university. But I did not know what I would major in. I had been granted my wish: one semester of philosophy. Any other subject would have done as well.

7)   Eva

ONCE DURING MY VACATION I visited the house where years before Demian had lived with his mother. I saw an old woman strolling in the garden and, speaking with her, learned that it was her house. I inquired after the Demian family. She remembered them very well but could not tell me where they lived at present. Sensing my interest she took me into the house, brought out a leather album and showed me a photo of Demian's mother. I could hardly remember what she looked like, but now as I saw the small likeness my heart stood still: it was my dream image! That was she, the tall, almost masculine woman who resembled her son, with maternal traits, severity, passion; beautiful and alluring, beautiful and unapproachable, *daemon* and mother, fate and beloved. There was no mistaking her!

To discover in this fashion that my dream image existed struck me as a miracle. So there was a woman who looked like that, who bore the features of my destiny! And to be Demian's mother. Where was she?

Shortly afterwards I embarked on my trip. What a strange journey it was! I traveled restlessly from place to place, following every impulse, always searching for this woman. There were days when everyone I met reminded me of her, echoed her, seemed to resemble her, drew me through the streets of unfamiliar cities, through railroad stations and into trains, as in an intricate dream. There were other days when I realized the futility of my search. Then I would idly sit somewhere in a park or in some hotel garden, in a waiting room, trying to make the picture come alive within me. But it had become shy and elusive. I found it impossible to fall asleep. Only while traveling on the train could I catch an occasional brief nap. Once, in Zurich, a woman approached me, an impudent pretty creature. I took hardly any notice of her and walked past as though she didn't exist. I would rather have died on the spot than have paid attention to another woman, even for an hour.

I felt my fate drawing me on, I felt the moment of my fulfillment coming near and I was sick with impatience at not being able to do anything. Once in a railroad station, in Innsbruck I think, I caught sight of a woman who reminded me of her—in a train just pulling away. I was miserable for days. And suddenly the form reappeared in a dream one night. I awoke humilated and dejected by the futility of my hunt and I took the next train home.

A few weeks later I enrolled at the university of H. I found everything disappointing. The lectures on the history of philosophy were just as uninspired and stereotyped as the activities of most of the students. Everything seemed to run according to an old pattern, everyone was doing the same thing, and the exaggerated gaiety on the boyish faces looked depressingly empty and ready-made. But at least I was free, I had the whole day to myself, lived quietly and peacefully in an old house near the town wall, and on my table lay a few volumes of Nietzsche. I lived with him, sensed the loneliness of his soul, perceived the fate that had propelled him on inexorably; I suffered with him, and rejoiced that there had been one man who had followed his destiny so relentlessly.

Late one evening I was sauntering through town. An autumn wind was blowing and I could hear the fraternities frolic in the taverns. Clouds of tobacco smoke drifted out open windows with a profusion of song, loud, rhythmic yet uninspired, lifelessly uniform.

I stood at a street corner and listened: out of two bars the methodically rehearsed gaiety of youth rang out against the night. False communion everywhere, everywhere shedding the responsibility of fate, flight to the herd for warmth.

Two men slowly walked past behind me. I caught a few words of their conversation.

"Isn't it just like the young men's house in a kraal?" said one of them. "Everything fits down to the tattooing which is in vogue again. Look, that's young Europe."

The voice sounded strangely and admonishingly familiar. I followed the two of them down the dark lane. One of them was a Japanese, small and elegant. Under a street lamp I saw his yellow face light up in a smile.

The other was now speaking again.

"I imagine it's just as bad where you come from, in Japan. People that don't follow the herd are rare everywhere. There are some here too."

I felt a mixture of alarm and joy at each word. I knew

the speaker. It was Demian. I followed him and the Japanese through the wind-swept streets; listening to their conversation I relished the sound of Demian's voice. It still had its familiar ring; the same old beautiful certainty and calm had all their old power over me. Now all was well. I had found him.

At the end of a street in the suburbs the Japanese took his leave and unlocked his house door. Demian retraced his steps, I had stopped and was waiting for him in the middle of the street. I became very agitated as I saw him approach, upright, with elastic step, in a brown rubber raincoat. He came closer without changing his pace until he stopped a few steps in front of me. Then he removed his hat and revealed his old light-skinned face with the decisive mouth and the peculiar brightness on his broad forehead.

"Demian," I called out.

He stretched out his hand.

"So, it's you, Sinclair! I was expecting you."

"Did you know I was here?"

"I didn't exactly know it but I definitely wished you were. I didn't catch sight of you until this evening. You've been following us for quite some time."

"Did you recognize me at once?"

"Of course. You've changed somewhat. But you have the sign."

"The sign. What kind of sign?"

"We used to call it the mark of Cain earlier on—if you can still remember. It's our sign. You've always had it, that's why I became your friend. But now it has become more distinct."

"I wasn't aware of that. Or actually, yes, once I painted

a picture of you, Demian, and was astonished that it also resembled myself. Was that the sign?"

"That was it. It's good that you're here. My mother will be pleased, too."

Suddenly I was frightened.

"Your mother? Is she here, too? But she doesn't know me."

"But she knows about you. She will recognize you even without my saying who you are. We've been in the dark about you for a long time."

"I often wanted to write you, but it was no use. I've known for some time that I would find you soon. I waited for it each day."

He thrust his arm under mine and walked along with me. An aura of calm surrounded him which affected me, too. Soon we were talking as we used to talk in the past. Our thoughts went back to our time in school, the Confirmation classes and also to that last unhappy meeting during my vacation. Only our earliest and closest bond, the Franz Kromer episode, was never mentioned.

Suddenly we found ourselves in the midst of a strange conversation touching on many ominous topics. Picking up where Demian left off in his conversation with the Japanese, we had discussed the life most of the students led, then came to something else, something that seemed to lie far afield. Yet in Demian's words an intimate connection became evident.

He spoke about the spirit of Europe and the signs of the times. Everywhere, he said, we could observe the reign of the herd instinct, nowhere freedom and love. All this false communion—from the fraternities to the choral societies and the nations themselves—was an inevitable development, was a community born of fear and dread, out of embarrassment, but inwardly rotten, outworn, close to collapsing.

"Genuine communion," said Demian, "is a beautiful thing. But what we see flourishing everywhere is nothing of the kind. The real spirit will come from the knowledge that separate individuals have of one another and for a time it will transform the world. The community spirit at present is only a manifestation of the herd instinct. Men fly into each other's arms because they are afraid of each other—the owners are for themselves, the workers for themselves, the scholars for themselves! And why are they afraid? You are only afraid if you are not in harmony with yourself. People are afraid because they have never owned up to themselves. A whole society composed of men afraid of the unknown within them! They all sense that the rules they live by are no longer valid, that they live according to archaic laws—neither their religion nor their morality is in any way suited to the needs of the present. For a hundred years or more Europe has done nothing but study and build factories! They know exactly how many ounces of powder it takes to kill a man but they don't know how to pray to God, they don't even know how to be happy for a single contented hour. Just take a look at a student dive! Or a resort where the rich congregate. It's hopeless. Dear Sinclair, nothing good can come of all of this. These people who huddle together in fear are filled with dread and malice, no one trusts the other. They hanker after ideals that are ideals no longer but they will hound the man to death who sets up a new one. I can feel the approaching conflict. It's coming, believe me, and soon. Of course it will not 'improve' the world. Whether the workers kill the manufacturers or whether Germany makes war on Russia will merely mean a change of ownership. But it won't have been entirely in vain. It will reveal the bankruptcy of present-day ideals, there will be a sweeping away of Stone Age gods. The world, as it is now, wants to die, wants to perish—and it will.

"And what will happen to us during this conflict?"

"To us? Oh, perhaps we'll perish in it. Our kind can be shot, too. Only we aren't done away with as easily as all that. Around what remains of us, around those of us who survive, the will of the future will gather. The will of humanity, which our Europe has shouted down for a time with its frenzy of technology, will come to the fore again. And then it will become clear that the will of humanity is nowhere—and never was—identical with the will of present-day societies, states and peoples, clubs and churches. No, what Nature wants of man stands indelibly written in the individual, in you, in me. It stood written in Jesus, it stood written in Nietzsche. These tendencies— which are the only important ones and which, of course, can assume different forms every day—will have room to breathe once the present societies have collapsed."

It was late when we stopped in front of a garden by the river.

"This is where we live," said Demian. "You must come visit us soon. We've been waiting for you."

Elated I walked the long way home through a night which had now turned chill. Here and there students were reeling noisily to their quarters. I had often marked the contrast between their almost ludicrous gaiety and my lonely existence, sometimes with scorn, sometimes with a feeling of deprivation. But never until today had I felt with as much calm and secret strength how little it mattered to me, how remote and dead this world was for me. I remembered civil servants in my home town, worthy old gentlemen who clung to the memories of their drunken university days as to keepsakes from paradise and fashioned a cult of their "vanished" student years as poets or other romantics fashion their childhood. It was the same everywhere! Everywhere they looked for "freedom" and "luck" in the past, out of sheer dread of their present responsibilities and future course. They drank and caroused for a few years and then they slunk away to become serious-minded gentlemen in the service of the state. Yes, our society was rotten, and these student stupidities were not so stupid, not so bad as a hundred other things.

By the time I reached my distant house and was preparing for bed, all these thoughts had vanished and my entire being clung expectantly to the great promise that this day had brought me. As soon as I wished, even tomorrow, I was to see Demian's mother. Let the students have their drunken orgies and tattoo their faces; the rotten world could await its destruction—for all I cared. I was waiting for one thing—to see my fate step forth in a new guise.

I slept deeply until late in the morning. The new day dawned for me like a solemn feast, the kind I had not experienced since childhood. I was full of a great restlessness, yet without fear of any kind. I felt that an important day had begun for me and I saw and experienced the changed world around me, expectant, meaningful, and solemn; even the gentle autumn rain had its beauty and a calm and festive air full of happy, sacred music. For the first time the outer world was perfectly attuned to the world within; it was a joy to be alive. No house, no shop window, no face disturbed me, everything was as it should be, without any of the flat, humdrum look of the everyday; everything was a part of Nature, expectant and ready to face its destiny with reverence. That was how the world had appeared to me in the mornings when I was a small boy, on the great feast days, at Christmas or Easter. I had forgotten that the world could still be so lovely. I had grown accustomed to living within myself. I was re-signed to the knowledge that I had lost all appreciation of the outside world, that the loss of its bright colors was an inseparable part of the loss of my childhood, and that, in a certain sense, one had to pay for freedom and maturity of the soul with the renunciation of this cherished aura. But now, overjoyed, I saw that all this had only been buried or clouded over and that it was still possible—even if you had become liberated and had renounced your childhood happiness—to see the world shine and to savor the deli-cious thrill of the child's vision.

The moment came when I found my way back to the garden at the edge of town where I had taken leave of Demian the night before. Hidden behind tall, wet trees stood a little house, bright and livable. Tall plants flow-ered behind plate glass; behind glistening windows dark walls shone with pictures and rows of books. The front door led straight into a small, warm hallway. A silent old maid, dressed in black with a white apron, showed me in and took my coat.

She left me alone in the hallway. I looked around and at once was swept into the middle of my dream. High up on the dark wood-paneled wall, above a door, hung a familiar painting, my bird with the golden-yellow sparrow hawk's head, clambering out of the terrestrial shell. Deeply moved, I stood there motionless—I felt joy and pain as though at this moment everything I had ever done and experienced returned to me in the form of a reply and fulfillment. In a flash I saw hosts of images throng past my mind's eye: my parents' house with the old coat of arms above the doorway, the boy Demian sketching the emblem, myself as a boy under the fearful spell of my enemy Kromer, myself as an adolescent in my room at school painting my dream bird at a quiet table, the soul caught in the intricacies of its own threads—and everything, everything to this present moment resounded once more within me, was affirmed by me, answered, sanctioned.

With tears in my eyes I stared at my picture and read within myself. Then I lowered my eyes: beneath the painting of the bird in the open door stood a tall woman in a dark dress. It was she.

I was unable to utter a word. With a face that resembled her son's, timeless, ageless, and full of inner strength, the beautiful woman smiled with dignity. Her gaze was fulfillment, her greeting a homecoming. Silently I stretched my hands out to her. She took both of them in her firm, warm hands.

"You are Sinclair. I recognized you at once. Welcome!"

Her voice was deep and warm. I drank it up like sweet wine. And now I looked up and into her quiet face, the black unfathomable eyes, at her fresh, ripe lips, the clear, regal brow that bore the sign.

"How glad I am," I said and kissed her hands. "I believe I have been on my way my whole life—and now I have come home."

She smiled like a mother.

"One never reaches home," she said. "But where paths that have affinity for each other intersect the whole world looks like home, for a time."

She was expressing what I had felt on my way to her. Her voice and her words resembled her son's and yet were quite different. Everything was riper, warmer, more self-evident. But just as Max had never given anyone the impression of being a boy, so his mother did not appear at all like a woman who had a full-grown son, so young and sweet were her face and hair, so taut and smooth her golden skin, so fresh her mouth. More regal even than in my dreams she stood before me.

This, then, was the new guise in which my fate revealed itself to me, no longer stern, no longer setting me apart, but fresh and joyful! I made no resolutions, took no vows —I had attained a goal, a high point on the road: from there the next stage of the journey appeared unhampered and marvelous, leading toward promised lands. Whatever might happen to me now, I was filled with ecstasy: that this woman existed in the world, that I could drink in her voice and breathe her presence. No matter whether she would become my mother, my beloved or a goddess— if she could just be here! if only my path would be close to hers!

She pointed up to my painting.

"You never made Max happier than with this picture," she said thoughtfully. "And me, too. We were waiting for you and when the painting came we knew that you were on your way. When you were a little boy, Sinclair, my son one day came home from school and said to me: there is a boy in school, he has the sign on his brow, he has to become my friend. That was you. You have not had an easy time but we had confidence in you. You met Max again during one of your vacations. You must have been about sixteen at the time. Max told me about it—"

I interrupted: "He told you about that? That was the most miserable period of my life!"

"Yes, Max said to me: Sinclair has the most difficult part coming now. He's making one more attempt to take refuge among the others. He's even begun going to bars. But he won't succeed. His sign is obscured but it sears him secretly. Wasn't it like that?"

"Yes, exactly. Then I found Beatrice and I finally found a master again. His name was Pistorius. Only then did it become clear to me why my boyhood had been so closely bound up with Max and why I could not free myself from him. Dear mother, at that time I often thought that I should have to take my life. Is the way as difficult as this for everybody?"

She stroked my hair. The touch felt as light as a breeze.

"It is always difficult to be born. You know the chick does not find it easy to break his way out of the shell. Think back and ask yourself: Was the way all that difficult? Was it only difficult? Wasn't it beautiful, too? Can you think of a more beautiful and easier way?"

I shook my head.

"It was difficult," I said as though I were asleep, "it was hard until the dream came."

She nodded and pierced me with a glance.

"Yes, you must find your dream, then the way becomes easy. But there is no dream that lasts forever, each dream is followed by another, and one should not cling to any particular one."

I was startled and frightened. Was that a warning, a defensive gesture, so soon? But it didn't matter: I was prepared to let her guide me and not to inquire into goals.

"I do not know," I said, "how long my dream is supposed to last. I wish it could be forever. My fate has received me under the picture of the bird like a lover and like a beloved. I belong to my fate and to no one else."

"As long as the dream is your fate you should remain faithful to it," she confirmed in a serious tone of voice.

I was overcome by sadness and a longing to die in this enchanted hour. I felt tears—what an infinity since I had last wept—well up irresistibly in my eyes and overwhelm me. I turned abruptly away from her, stepped to the window, and stared blindly into the distance.

I heard her voice behind me, calm and yet brimful with tenderness as a beaker with wine.

"Sinclair, you are a child! Your fate loves you. One day it will be entirely yours—just as you dream it—if you remain constant to it."

I had gained control of myself and turned toward her again. She gave me her hand.

"I have a few friends," she said with a smile, "a few very close friends who call me Frau Eva. You shall be one of them if you wish."

She led me to the door, opened it, and pointed into the garden. "You'll find Max out there."

I stood dazed and shaken under the tall trees, not knowing whether I was more awake or more in a dream than ever. The rain dripped gently from the branches. Slowly I walked out into the garden that extended some way along the river. Finally I found Demian. He was standing in an open summer house, stripped to the waist, punching a suspended sandbag.

I stopped, astonished. Demian looked strikingly handsome with his broad chest, and firm, manly features; the raised arms with taut muscles were strong and capable, the movements sprang playfully and smoothly from hips, shoulders, and wrists.

"Demian," I called out. "What are you doing there?"

He laughed happily.

"Practicing. I've promised the Japanese a boxing match, the little fellow is as agile as a cat and, of course, just as sly, but he won't be able to beat me. There's a very slight humiliation for which I have to pay him back."

He put on his shirt and coat.

"You've seen my mother?" he asked.

"Yes, Demian, what a wonderful mother you have! Frau Eva! The name fits her perfectly. She *is* like a universal mother."

For a moment he looked thoughtfully into my face.

"So you know her name already? You can be proud of yourself. You are the first person she has told it to during the first meeting."

From this day on I went in and out of the house like a son or brother—but also as someone in love. As soon as I opened the gate, as soon as I caught sight of the tall trees in the garden, I felt happy and rich. Outside was reality: streets and houses, people and institutions, libraries and lecture halls—but here inside was love; here lived the legend and the dream. And yet we lived in no way cut off from the outside world; in our thoughts and conversations we often lived in the midst of it, only on an entirely different plane. We were not separated from the majority of men by a boundary but simply by another mode of vision. Our task was to represent an island in the world, a proto-type perhaps, or at least a prospect of a different way of life. I, who had been isolated for so long, learned about the companionship which is possible between people who have tasted complete loneliness. I never again hankered after the tables of the fortunate and the feasts of the blessed. Never again did envy or nostalgia overcome me when I witnessed the collective pleasures of others. And gradually I was initiated into the secret of those who wear the sign in their faces.

We who wore the sign might justly be considered "odd" by the world; yes, even crazy, and dangerous. We were *aware* or in the process of becoming aware and our striving was directed toward achieving a more and more complete state of awareness while the striving of the others was a quest aimed at binding their opinions, ideals, duties, their lives and fortunes more and more closely to those of the herd. There, too, was striving, there, too, were power and greatness. But whereas we, who were marked, believed that we represented the will of Nature to something new, to the individualism of the future, the others sought to perpetuate the status quo. Humanity—which they loved as we did—was for them something complete that must be maintained and protected. For us, humanity was a distant goal toward which all men were moving, whose image no one knew, whose laws were nowhere written down.

Apart from Frau Eva, Max, and myself, various other seekers were more or less closely attached to the circle. Quite a few had set out on very individual paths, had set themselves quite unusual goals, and clung to specific ideas and duties. They included astrologers and cabalists, also a disciple of Count Tolstoi, and all kinds of delicate, shy, and vulnerable creatures, followers of new sects, devotees of Indian asceticism, vegetarians, and so forth. We actually had no mental bonds in common save the respect which each one accorded the ideals of the other. Those with whom we felt a close kinship were concerned with mankind's past search for gods and ideals—their studies often reminded me of Pistorius. They brought books with them, translated aloud texts in ancient languages, showed us illustrations of ancient symbols and rites and taught us to see how humanity's entire store of ideals so far consisted of dreams that had emanated from the unconscious, of dreams in which humanity groped after its intimations of future potentialities. Thus we became acquainted with the wonderful thousand-headed tangle of gods from prehistory to the dawn of the Christian conversion. We heard the creeds of solitary holy men, of the transformations religions undergo in their migrations from one people to another. Thus, from everything we collected in this manner, we gained a critical understanding of our time and of contemporary Europe: with prodigious efforts mighty new weapons had been created for mankind but the end was flagrant, deep desolation of the spirit. Europe had conquered the whole world only to lose her own soul.

Our circle also included believers, adherents of certain hopes and healing faiths. There were Buddhists who sought to convert Europe, a disciple of Tolstoi who preached nonresistance to evil, as well as other sects. We in the inner circle listened but accepted none of these teachings as anything but metaphors. We, who bore the mark, felt no anxiety about the shape the future was to take. All of these faiths and teachings seemed to us already dead and useless. The only duty and destiny we acknowledged was that each one of us should become so completely himself, so utterly faithful to the active seed which Nature planted within him, that in living out its growth he could be surprised by nothing unknown to come.

Although we might not have been able to express it, we all felt distinctly that a new birth amid the collapse of this present world was imminent, already discernible. Demian often said to me: "What will come is beyond imagining. The soul of Europe is a beast that has lain fettered for an infinitely long time. And when it's free, its first movements won't be the gentlest. But the means are unimportant if only the real needs of the soul—which has for so long been repeatedly stunted and anesthetized— come to light. Then our day will come, then we will be needed. Not as leaders and lawgivers—we won't be there to see the new laws—but rather as those who are willing, as men who are ready to go forth and stand prepared wherever fate may need them. Look, all men are prepared to accomplish the incredible if their ideals are threatened. But no one is ready when a new ideal, a new and perhaps dangerous and ominous impulse, makes itself felt. The few who will be ready at that time and who will go forth —will be us. That is why we are marked—as Cain was —to arouse fear and hatred and drive men out of a confining idyl into more dangerous reaches. All men who have had an effect on the course of human history, all of them without exception, were capable and effective only because they were ready to accept the inevitable. It is true of Moses and Buddha, of Napoleon and Bismarck. What particular movement one serves and what pole one is directed from are matters outside one's own choice. If Bismarck had understood the Social Democrats and compromised with them he would have merely been shrewd but no man of destiny. The same applies to Napoleon, Caesar, Loyola, all men of that species in fact. Always, you must think of these things in evolutionary, in historical terms! When the upheavals of the earth's surface flung the creatures of the sea onto the land and the land creatures into the sea, the specimens of the various orders that were ready to follow their destiny were the ones that accomplished the new and unprecedented; by making new biological adjustments they were able to save their species from destruction. We do not know whether these were the same specimens that had previously distinguished themselves among their fellows as conservative, upholders of the status quo, or rather as eccentrics, revolutionaries; but we do know they were ready, and could therefore lead their species into new phases of evolution. That is why we want to be *ready*."

Frau Eva was often present during these conversations yet she did not participate in quite the same manner. She was a listener, full of trust and understanding, an echo for each one of us who explained his thoughts. It seemed as though all thinking emanated from her and in the end went back to her. My happiness consisted in sitting near her, hearing her voice occasionally and sharing the rich, soulful atmosphere surrounding her.

She was immediately aware of any change, any unhappiness or new development within me. It even seemed to me that my dreams at night were inspired by her. I would often recount them to her and she found them comprehensible and natural; there was no unusual turn in them that she could not follow. For a time my dreams repeated patterns of our daytime conversations. I dreamed that the whole world was in turmoil and that by myself, or with Demian, I was tensely waiting for the great moment. The face of fate remained obscured but somehow bore the features of Frau Eva: to be chosen or spurned by her, that was fate.

Sometimes she would say with a smile: "Your dream is incomplete, Sinclair. You've left out the best part." And then I would remember the part I had left out and not understand how I could have forgotten it.

At times I was dissatisfied with myself and tortured with desire: I believed I could no longer bear to have her near me without taking her in my arms. She sensed this, too, at once. Once when I had stayed away for several days and returned bewildered she took me aside and said: "You must not give way to desires which you don't believe in. I know what you desire. You should, however, either be capable of renouncing these desires or feel wholly justified in having them. Once you are able to make your request in such a way that you will be quite certain of its fulfillment, then the fulfillment will come. But at present you alternate between desire and renunciation and are afraid all the time. All that must be overcome. Let me tell you a story."

And she told me about a youth who had fallen in love with a planet. He stood by the sea, stretched out his arms and prayed to the planet, dreamed of it, and directed all his thoughts to it. But he knew, or felt he knew, that a star cannot be embraced by a human being. He considered it to be his fate to love a heavenly body without any hope of fulfillment and out of this insight he constructed an entire philosophy of renunciation and silent, faithful suffering that would improve and purify him. Yet all his dreams reached the planet. Once he stood again on the high cliff at night by the sea and gazed at the planet and burned with love for it. And at the height of his longing he leaped into the emptiness toward the planet, but at the instant of leaping "it's impossible" flashed once more through his mind. There he lay on the shore, shattered. He had not understood how to love. If at the instant of leaping he had had the strength of faith in the fulfillment of his love he would have soared into the heights and been united with the star.

"Love must not entreat," she added, "or demand. Love must have the strength to become certain within itself. Then it ceases merely to be attracted and begins to attract. Sinclair, your love is attracted to me. Once it begins to attract me, I will come. I will not make a gift of myself, I must be won."

Another time she told me a different story, concerning a lover whose love was unrequited. He withdrew completely within himself, believing his love would consume him. The world became lost to him, he no longer noticed blue sky and green woods, he no longer heard the brook murmur; his ears had turned deaf to the notes of the harp: nothing mattered any more; he had become poor and wretched. Yet his love increased and he would rather have died or been ruined than renounce possessing this beautiful woman. Then he felt that his passion had consumed everything else within him and become so strong, so magnetic that the beautiful woman must follow. She

came to him and he stood with outstretched arms ready to
draw her to him. As she stood before him she was completely transformed and with awe he felt and saw that he
had won back all he had previously lost. She stood before
him and surrendered herself to him and sky, forest, and
brook all came toward him in new and resplendent colors,
belonged to him, and spoke to him in his own language.
And instead of merely winning a woman he embraced
the entire world and every star in heaven glowed within
him and sparkled with joy in his soul. He had loved and
had found himself. But most people love to lose themselves.

My love for Frau Eva seemed to fill my whole life. But
every day it manifested itself differently. Sometimes I felt
certain that it was not she as a person whom I was attracted to and yearned for with all my being, but that she
existed only as a metaphor of my inner self, a metaphor
whose sole purpose was to lead me more deeply into myself. Things she said often sounded like replies from my
subconscious to questions that tormented me. There were
other moments when I sat beside her and burned with
sensual desire and kissed objects she had touched. And
little by little, sensual and spiritual love, reality and sym-
bol began to overlap. Then it would happen that as I
thought about her in my room at home in tranquil intimacy I felt her hand in mine and her lips touching my
lips. Or I would be at her house, would look into her face
and hear her voice, yet not know whether she was real or
a dream. I began to sense how one can possess a love
constantly and eternally. I would have an insight while
reading a book—and this would feel the same as Eva's
kiss. She caressed my hair and smiled at me affectionately

and this felt like taking a step forward within myself. Everything significant and full of fate for me adopted her form. She could transform herself into any of my thoughts and each of my thoughts could be transformed into her.

I had been apprehensive about the Christmas vacation —to be spent at my parents' house—because I thought it would be agony to be away from Frau Eva for two whole weeks. But it did not turn out like that. It was wonderful to be at home and yet be able to think of her. When I arrived back in H. I waited two more days before going to see her, so as to savor this security, this being independent of her physical presence. I had dreams, too, in which my union with her was consummated in new symbolic acts. She was an ocean into which I streamed. She was a star and I another on my way to her, circling round each other. I told her this dream when I first visited her again.

"The dream is beautiful," she said quietly. "Make it come true."

There came a day in early spring that I have never forgotten. I entered the hallway, a window was open and a stream of air let in the heavy fragrance of the hyacinths. As no one was about, I went upstairs to Max Demian's study. I tapped lightly on the door and, as was my custom, went in without waiting for a reply.

The room was dark, all the curtains were drawn. The door to the small adjoining room stood open. There Max had set up a chemical laboratory. That's where the only light came from. I thought no one was in and drew back one of the curtains.

Then I saw Max slumped on a stool by the curtained window, looking oddly changed, and it flashed through

me: You've seen this before! His arms hung limp, hands in
his lap, his head bent slightly forward, and his eyes,
though open, were unseeing and dead; in one of his pupils
as in a piece of glass a thin, harsh ray of light snapped the
iris open and shut, open and shut. The wan face was ab-
sorbed in itself and without expression, except for its immense rigidity; he resembled an age-old animal mask at
the portal of a temple. He did not seem to breathe.

Overcome by dread I quietly left the room and walked
downstairs. In the hallway I met Frau Eva, pale and
seemingly tired, which I had never known her to be before. Just then a shadow passed over the window, the
white glare of the sun suddenly fled.

"I was in Max's room," I whispered rapidly. "Has something happened? He's either asleep or lost within himself,
I don't know which; I saw him look like that once before."

"You didn't wake him, did you?" she quickly asked.

"No. He didn't hear me. I left the room immediately.
Tell me, what is the matter with him?"

She swept the back of her hand once across her brow.

"Don't worry, Sinclair, nothing will happen to him. He
has withdrawn. It will soon pass."

She stood up and went out into the garden—although it
was beginning to rain. I felt that she did not want me to
accompany her and so I walked up and down the hallway,
inhaled the bewildering scent of the hyacinths, stared at
my bird picture above the doorway, and breathed the
stifling atmosphere that filled the house that morning.
What was it? What had happened?

Frau Eva returned before long. Raindrops clung to her
black hair. She sat down in her armchair. She seemed
weary. I stepped up to her, bent over her head, and kissed

the rain out of her hair. Her eyes were bright and calm but the raindrops tasted like tears.

"Should I go and see how he is?" I asked in a whisper. She smiled weakly.

"Don't be a little boy, Sinclair!" she admonished me, loudly as though trying to break a spell within herself. "Get along now and come back later. I can't talk to you now."

I half walked, half ran from the house and the town, toward the mountains. The fine rain slanted into my face, low clouds swept by as though weighed down with fear. Near the ground there was hardly a breath of air but in the higher altitudes a storm seemed to rage. Several times the lurid sun broke briefly through harsh rifts in the steel-gray clouds.

Then a loose, yellow cloud swept across the sky, collided with the other, gray bank of cloud. In a few seconds the wind had fashioned a shape out of this yellow and blue-gray mass, a gigantic bird that tore itself free of the steel-blue chaos and flew off into the sky with a great beating of wings. Then the storm became audible and rain rattled down mixed with hail. A brief, incredible, terrifying roar of thunder cracked across the rain-lashed landscape and immediately afterwards a gleam of sunshine burst through. On the nearby mountains the pale snow shone livid and unreal above the brown forest.

When, hours later, I returned wet and wind-blown, Demian himself opened the door.

He took me up to his room. A gas jet was burning in his laboratory and papers were strewn about the floor. He had evidently been working.

"Sit down," he invited, "you must be exhausted, it was

horrible weather. One can see that you really were outside. There'll be tea in a moment."

"Something is the matter today," I began hesitantly. "It
can't only be a thunderstorm."

He looked at me inquiringly.

"Did you see something?"

"Yes. I saw a picture in the clouds, quite clearly for a
moment."

"What kind of picture?"

"It was a bird."

"The sparrow hawk? Your dream bird?"

"Yes, it was my sparrow hawk. It was yellow and gigantic and it flew off into the blue-black clouds."

Demian heaved a great sigh.

There was a knock on the door. The old servant brought
in the tea.

"Help yourself, Sinclair, please. I don't believe you saw
the bird just by chance."

"By chance? Does one get to see such things by
chance?"

"Quite right. No, one doesn't. The bird has a significance. Do you know what?"

"No. I only feel that it signifies some shattering event, a
move on the part of destiny. I believe that it concerns all
of us."

He was pacing excitedly back and forth.

"A move on the part of destiny!" he shouted. "I
dreamed the same kind of thing last night and my mother
had a presentiment yesterday which conveyed the same
message. I dreamed I was climbing up a ladder placed
against a tree trunk or tower. When I reached the top I
saw the whole landscape ablaze—a vast plain with in-

numerable towns and villages. I can't tell you the whole dream yet, everything is still somewhat confused."

"Do you feel that the dream concerns you personally?"

"Of course. No one dreams anything that doesn't 'concern him personally.' But it doesn't concern me only, you're right. I differentiate quite sharply between dreams that reveal movements within my own soul and the other, far rarer dreams in which the fate of all mankind suggests itself. I have rarely had such dreams and never before one of which I could say that it was a prophecy which was fulfilled. The interpretations are too uncertain. But I know for sure that I have dreamed something that doesn't concern me alone. For this dream links up with others, previous dreams I have had, to which it is a sequel. These are the dreams, Sinclair, which fill me with the forebodings I've spoken of to you. We both know that the world is quite rotten but that wouldn't be any reason to predict its imminent collapse or something of the kind. But for several years I have had dreams from which I conclude, or which make me feel, that the collapse of an old world is indeed imminent. At first these were weak and remote intimations but they have become increasingly stronger and more distinct. I still know nothing except that *something* is going to happen on a vast scale, something dreadful in which I myself will be involved. Sinclair, we will take part in this event that we have discussed so often. The world wants to renew itself. There's a smell of death in the air. Nothing can be born without first dying. But it is far more terrible than I had thought."

I stared at him aghast.

"Can't you tell me the rest of your dream?" I asked shyly.

He shook his head.

"No."

The door opened to let in Frau Eva.

"You're not feeling sad, I hope."

She looked refreshed, all trace of fatigue had vanished. Demian smiled at her and she came up to us as a mother approaches frightened children.

"No, we are not sad, mother. We've merely tried to puzzle out these new omens. But it's no use anyway. Whatever happens will suddenly be here; then we shall learn soon enough what we need to know."

But I felt dispirited, and when I took my leave and walked alone through the hallway, the stale scent of the hyacinths seemed cadaverous. A shadow had fallen over us.

8)   The End Begins

I HAD PERSUADED my parents to allow me the summer
semester in H. My friends and I now spent almost all our
time in the garden by the river instead of the house. The
Japanese, who had been duly beaten in the boxing match,
had departed; the disciple of Tolstoi had gone, too.
Demian kept a horse and went for long rides day after
day. I was frequently alone with his mother.

There were times when I was simply astonished how
peaceful my life had become. I had so long been accustomed to being alone, to leading a life of self-denial, to
battling strenuously with my agonizing difficulties, that
these months in H. seemed to me altogether like a magic
dream island on which I was allowed to lead a comfortable, enchanted existence among beautiful and agreeable
surroundings. I had a presentiment that this was a foretaste of that new and higher community which we speculated about so much. Yet at any moment this happiness
could produce in me the deepest melancholy, for I knew
very well that it could not last. It was not my lot to breathe

fullness and comfort, I needed the spur of tormented haste. I felt that one day I would waken from these beloved images of beauty and stand, alone again, in the cold world where there was nothing for me but solitude and struggle—neither peace nor relaxation, no easy living together.

At those moments I would nestle with redoubled affection close to Frau Eva, glad that my fate still bore these beautiful calm features.

The summer weeks passed quickly and uneventfully, the semester was nearly over and it would soon be time for me to leave. I dared not think of it, but clung to each beautiful day as the butterfly clings to his honeyed flower. This had been my happy time, life's first fulfillment, my acceptance into this intimate, elect circle—what was to follow? I would battle through again, suffer the old longings, dream dreams, be alone.

One day foreboding came over me with such force that my love for Frau Eva suddenly flared up painful within me. My God, how soon I must leave here, see her no more, no longer hear her dear assured steps throughout the house, no longer find her flowers on my table! And what had I achieved? I had dreamed, had luxuriated in dreams and contentment, instead of winning her, instead of struggling to clasp her forever to myself! Everything she had told me about genuine love came back to me, a hundred delicate admonitions, as many gentle enticements, promises perhaps—what had I made of them? Nothing. Absolutely nothing!

I went to the center of my room and stood still, endeavoring to concentrate the whole of my consciousness on Frau Eva, summoning all the strength in my soul to let her feel my love and draw her to me. She must come, she must long for my embrace, my kiss must tremble insatiably on her ripe lips.

I stood and concentrated every energy until I could feel cold creeping up my fingers and toes. I felt strength radiating from me. For a few moments I felt something contract within me, something bright and cool which felt like a crystal in my heart—I knew it was my ego. The chill crept up to my chest.

Relaxed from this terrible tension I felt that something was about to happen. I was mortally exhausted but I was ready to behold Eva step into the room, radiant and ecstatic.

The clattering of hooves could be heard approaching along the street. It sounded near and metallic, then suddenly stopped. I leaped to the window and saw Demian dismounting below. I ran down.

"What is it, Demian?"

He paid no attention to my words. He was very pale and sweat poured down his cheeks. He tied the bridle of his steaming horse to the garden fence and took my arm and walked down the street with me.

"Have you heard about it?"

I had heard nothing.

Demian squeezed my arm and turned his face toward me, with a strangely somber yet sympathetic look in his eyes.

"Yes, it's starting. You've heard about the difficulties with Russia."

"What? Is it war?"

He spoke very softly although no one was anywhere near us.

"It hasn't been declared yet. But there will be war. You can take my word for that. I didn't want to worry you but I have seen omens on three different occasions since that time. So it won't be the end of the world, no earthquake, no revolution, but war. You'll see what a sensation that will be! People will love it. Even now they can hardly wait for the killing to begin—their lives are that dull! But you will see, Sinclair, that this is only the beginning. Perhaps it will be a very big war, a war on a gigantic scale. But that, too, will only be the beginning. The new world has begun and the new world will be terrible for those clinging to the old. What will you do?"

I was dumfounded, it all sounded so strange, so improbable.

"I don't know—and you?"

He shrugged his shoulders.

"I'll be called up as soon as the mobilization order comes through. I'm a lieutenant."

"You, a lieutenant! I had no idea."

"Yes, that was one of the ways I compromised. You know I dislike calling attention to myself so much I almost always went to the other extreme, just to give a correct impression. I believe I'll be on the front in a week."

"My God."

"Now don't get sentimental. Of course it's not going to be any fun ordering men to fire on living beings, but that will be incidental. Each of us will be caught up in the great chain of events. You, too, you'll be drafted, for sure."

"And what about your mother, Demian?"

Only now my thoughts turned back to what had happened a quarter of an hour before. How the world had changed in the meantime! I had summoned all my strength to conjure up the sweetest of images and now fate looked at me suddenly with a threatening and horrible mask.

"My mother? We don't have to worry about her. She is safe, safer than anyone else in the world today. Do you love her that much?"

"Didn't you know?"

He laughed lightly, relieved.

"Of course I knew. No one has called my mother Frau Eva who hasn't been in love with her. You either called me or her today."

"Yes, I called her."

"She felt it. She sent me away all of a sudden, saying I would have to go see you. I had just told her the news about Russia."

We turned around and exchanged a few words more. Demian untied his horse and mounted.

Only upstairs in my room did I realize how much Demian's news, and still more the previous strain, had exhausted me. But Frau Eva had heard me! My thoughts had reached her heart. She would have come herself— if . . . How curious all this was, and, fundamentally, how beautiful! And now there was to be war. What we had talked about so often was to begin. Demian had known so much about it ahead of time. How strange that the stream of the world was not to bypass us any more, that it now went straight through our hearts, and that now or very soon the moment would come when the world would need us, when it would seek to transform itself. Demian was right, one could not be sentimental about that. The only remarkable thing was that I was to share the very personal matter of my fate with so many others, with the whole world in fact. Well, so be it!

I was prepared. When I walked through town in the evening every street corner was buzzing, everywhere the word was *war*.

I went to Frau Eva's. We ate supper in the summer house. I was the only guest. No one said a word about the war. Only later on, shortly before I was to leave, Frau Eva said: "Dear Sinclair, you called me today. You know why I didn't come myself. But don't forget: you know the call now and whenever you need someone who bears the sign, you can appeal to me."

She rose to her feet and preceded me into the garden twilight. Tall and regal she strode between the silent trees.

I am coming to the end of my story. Everything went very rapidly from then on. Soon there was war, and Demian, strangely unfamiliar in his uniform, left us. I accompanied his mother home. It was not long before I, too, took my leave of her. She kissed me on the mouth and clasped me for a moment to her breast. Her great eyes burned close and firmly into mine.

All men seemed to have become brothers—overnight. They talked of "the fatherland" and of "honor," but what lay behind it was their own fate whose unveiled face they had now all beheld for one brief moment. Young men left their barracks, were packed into trains, and on many faces I saw a sign—not ours—but a beautiful, dignified sign nonetheless that meant love and death. I, too, was embraced by people whom I had never seen before and I understood this gesture and responded to it. Intoxication made them do it, not a hankering after their destiny. But this intoxication was sacred, for it was the result of their all having thrown that brief and terribly disquieting glance into the eyes of their fate.

It was nearly winter when I was sent to the front. Despite the excitement of being under fire for the first time, in the beginning everything disappointed me. At one time I had given much thought to why men were so very rarely capable of living for an ideal. Now I saw that many, no, all men were capable of dying for one. Yet it could not be a personal, a freely chosen ideal; it had to be one mutually accepted.

As time went on though I realized I had underestimated these men. However much mutual service and danger made a uniform mass of them, I still saw many approach the will of fate with great dignity. Many, very many, not only during the attack but at every moment of the day, wore in their eyes the remote, resolute, somewhat possessed look which knows nothing of aims and signified complete surrender to the incredible. Whatever they might think or believe, they were ready, they could be used, they were the clay of which the future could be shaped. The more single-mindedly the world concentrated on war and heroism, on honor and other old ideals, the more remote and improbable any whisper of genuine humanity sounded—that was all just surface, in the same way that the question of the war's external and political objectives remained superficial. Deep down, underneath, something was taking shape. Something akin to a new humanity. For I could see many men—and many died beside me—who had begun to feel acutely that hatred

and rage, slaughter and annihilation, were not bound up
with these objectives. No, these objectives and aims were
completely fortuitous. The most primitive, even the wild-
est feelings were not directed at the enemy; their bloody
task was merely an irradiation of the soul, of the soul
divided within itself, which filled them with the lust to
rage and kill, annihilate and die so that they might be
born anew.

One night in early spring I stood guard in front of a
farm that we had occupied. A listless wind was blowing
fitfully; across the Flemish sky cloud armies rode on high,
somewhere behind them the suggestion of a moon. I had
been uneasy the entire day—something was worrying me
deeply. Now on my dark guard post I fervently recalled
the images of my life and thought of Frau Eva and of
Demian. I stood braced against a poplar tree staring into
the drifting clouds whose mysteriously writhing patches
of light soon metamorphosed into huge series of swirling
images. From the strange weakness of my pulse, the in-
sensitiveness of my skin to wind and rain, and my intense
state of consciousness I could sense that a master was near
me.

A huge city could be seen in the clouds out of which
millions of people streamed in a host over vast landscapes.
Into their midst stepped a mighty, godlike figure, as huge
as a mountain range, with sparkling stars in her hair, bearing the features of Frau Eva. The ranks of the people
were swallowed up into her as into a giant cave and vanished from sight. The goddess cowered on the ground, the
mark luminous on her forehead. A dream seemed to hold
sway over her: she closed her eyes and her countenance
became twisted with pain. Suddenly she cried out and

from her forehead sprang stars, many thousands of shining stars that leaped in marvelous arches and semicircles across the black sky.

One of these stars shot straight toward me with a clear ringing sound and it seemed to seek me out. Then it burst asunder with a roar into a thousand sparks, tore me aloft and smashed me back to the ground again, the world shattered above me with a thunderous roar.

They found me near the poplar tree, covered with earth and with many wounds.

I lay in a cellar, guns roared above me. I lay in a wagon and jolted across the empty fields. Mostly I was asleep or unconscious. But the more deeply I slept the more strongly I felt that something was drawing me on, that I was following a force that had mastery over me.

I lay in a stable, on straw. It was dark and someone had stepped on my hand. But something inside me wanted to keep going and I was drawn on more forcefully than ever. Again I lay in a wagon and later on a stretcher or ladder. More strongly than ever I felt myself being summoned somewhere, felt nothing but this urge that I must finally get there.

Then I reached my goal. It was night and I was fully conscious. I had just felt the urge pulling mightily within me: now I was in a long hall, bedded down on the floor. I felt I had reached the destination which had summoned me. I turned my head: close to my mattress lay another; someone on it bent forward and looked at me. He had the sign on his forehead. It was Max Demian.

I was unable to speak and he could not or did not want to either. He just looked at me. The light from a bulb strung on the wall above him played down on his face. He smiled.

He gazed into my eyes for what seemed an endless time. Slowly he brought his face closer to mine: we almost touched.

"Sinclair," he said in a whisper.

I told him with a glance that I heard.

He smiled again, almost as with pity.

"Little fellow," he said, smiling.

His lips lay very close to mine. Quietly he continued to speak.

"Can you remember Franz Kromer?" he asked.

I blinked at him and smiled, too.

"Little Sinclair, listen: I will have to go away. Perhaps you'll need me again sometime, against Kromer or something. If you call me then I won't come crudely, on horseback or by train. You'll have to listen within yourself, then you will notice that I am within you. Do you understand? And something else. Frau Eva said that if ever you were in a bad way I was to give you a kiss from her that she sends by me. . . . Close your eyes, Sinclair!"

I closed my eyes in obedience. I felt a light kiss on my lips where there was always a little fresh blood which never would go away. And then I fell asleep.

Next morning someone woke me: I had to have my wounds dressed. When I was finally wide awake I turned quickly to the mattress next to mine. On it lay a stranger I'd never seen before.

Dressing the wound hurt. Everything that has happened to me since has hurt. But sometimes when I find the key and climb deep into myself where the images of fate lie aslumber in the dark mirror, I need only bend over that dark mirror to behold my own image, now completely resembling him, my brother, my master.

About the Author

Born in 1877 in Calw, on the edge of the Black Forest, Hermann Hesse was brought up in a missionary household where it was assumed that he would study for the ministry. Hesse's religious crisis (which is often recorded in his novels) led to his fleeing from the Maulbronn seminary in 1891, an unsuccessful cure by a well-known theologian and faith healer, and an attempted suicide. After being expelled from high school, he worked in bookshops for several years—a usual occupation for budding German authors.

His first novel, *Peter Camenzind* (1904), describes a youth who leaves his Swiss mountain village to become a poet. This was followed by *Unterm Rad* (1906), the tale of a schoolboy totally out of touch with his contemporaries, who flees through different cities after his escape from school.

World War I came as a terrific shock, and Hesse joined the pacifist Romain Rolland in antiwar activities—not only writing antiwar tracts and novels, but editing two newspapers for German prisoners of war. During this period, Hesse's first marriage broke up (reflected or discussed outright in *Knulp* and *Rosshalde*), he studied the works of Freud, eventually underwent analysis with Jung, and was for a time a patient in a sanatorium.

In 1919 he moved permanently to Switzerland, and brought out *Demian*, which reflects his preoccupation with the workings of the subconscious and with psychoanalysis. The book was an enormous success, and made Hesse famous throughout Europe.

In 1922 he turned his attention to the East, which he had visited several times before the war, and wrote a novel about Buddha titled *Siddhartha*. In 1927 he wrote *Steppenwolf*, the account of a man torn between animal instincts and bourgeois respectability, and in 1930 he published *Narziss and Goldmund*, regarded as "Hesse's greatest novel" (*New York Times*), dealing with the friendship between two medieval priests, one contented with his religion, the other a wanderer endlessly in search of peace and salvation.

Journey to the East appeared in 1932, and there was no major work until 1943, when he brought out *Magister Ludi*, which won him the Nobel Prize in 1946. Until his death in 1962 he lived in seclusion in Montagnola, Switzerland.

For your reading pleasure...

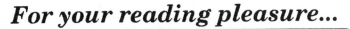